T0030963

ALSO BY

MAKI KASHIMADA

Touring the Land of the Dead

LOVE AT SIX THOUSAND DEGREES

Maki Kashimada

LOVE AT SIX THOUSAND DEGREES

Translated from the Japanese
by Haydn Trowell

Europa
editions

Europa Editions
27 Union Square West, Suite 302
New York, NY 10003
www.europaeditions.com
info@europaeditions.com

Original Japanese edition published by SHINCHOSHA Publishing Co., Ltd.
This English edition is published by arrangement with SHINCHOSHA Publishing Co., Ltd., Tokyo c/o Tuttle-Mori Agency, Inc., Tokyo
First publication 2023 by Europa Editions

Translation by Haydn Trowell
Original title: *6000-DO NO AI*

Library of Congress Cataloging in Publication Data is available
ISBN 978-1-60945-819-5

Kashimada, Maki
Love at Six Thousand Degrees

Art direction by Emanuele Ragnisco
instagram.com/emanueleragnisco

Cover design and illustration by Ginevra Rapisardi

Prepress by Grafica Punto Print – Rome

Printed in Canada

The woman stared into the confusion. Feeling as though she were about to strike upon something gravely abstract, she hurried to stop herself. Finally, she returned to her senses. She strained, trying to drag herself back to sanity. That effort wasn't trivial. Fine bubbles formed on the surface, breaking one after the next.

The curry in the stainless-steel pot was close to boiling. All that it needed was another five minutes. It was a sweet roux, for the child. The woman, her healthy and good husband, and their child, so young that there was as yet no telling whether he was destined to one day become a successful member of society. The curry was for the three of them. It was no more or less than that.

The child tugged at the woman's skirt. Mama, I'm hungry, he said. It's almost ready, the woman answered. I'm hungry, the child said again. The woman gave him a jelly, small enough that he could eat it in one mouthful. The child sucked it in.

Do you want to help? the woman asked. The child nodded. The woman handed him a ladle and lifted him up. Stir it gently, she said. The child turned the ladle with all his strength, creating a whirlpool. Mama, there are no potatoes, no onions. Where are they gone? The potatoes and onions, the woman replied, have melted away and disappeared. Why did they melt? the child asked. Because it's hot, the woman answered. When things get too hot, they melt away. People too, Mama? The woman lowered the child down to the floor. The child blinked. His face, illuminated by the light of the setting sun, was the color of burnt glass. The woman could hear the bugle of a door-to-door tofu merchant. You see now, the thing is, she began—but at that moment, the kitchen timer sounded. Startled, she turned off the stove. Mama, it's already five o'clock. When is Papa coming home? I wonder. Probably in about an hour, at six. When the woman heard the word *Papa*, she was struck by a sense of guilt. It was an inexplicable feeling. She couldn't remember. What had she been on the verge of laying bare to the child? She was always trying to tell him things that she hadn't been able to reveal even to her husband. But she had yet to realize that for herself.

Mama, can I watch TV? Alright. The woman, still wearing her apron, sat down in front of the television. She flicked through the channels to a children's program. There were costumed animals and a young man jumping up and down doing exercises. The child jumped up and down with them. The young man raised his arms into the air to do some stretches. He was wearing a sleeveless shirt. The woman stole a peek at his armpits. There was only a small amount of hair beneath them, fine and sparse as basting thread. His arms were as pale as a squid. He probably had very little body hair, the woman felt.

At that moment, the emergency bell in the woman's home—in other words, in her apartment complex—began to ring. Her body turned numb at that sound, and refused to move. The alarm made her feel agitated. It was prompting her to act quickly. And yet she couldn't move.

Mama, the child called out, tapping her on the shoulder. The chains holding her down relented. Mama, there's a fire! Let's run! We'll melt! We will, won't we? the woman answered. But we shouldn't panic. Let's go outside. It might all just be a mistake.

A crowd had gathered around the emergency bell by the

elevator. It was malfunctioning, a pregnant neighbor said to her. The woman felt as though her neighbor had gained an unfounded confidence ever since becoming pregnant. Before that, she had been so timid and shy that she would never have ventured to call out to her. I thought there was a fire, and so practically ran all the way out here. What a surprise! The neighbor laughed as she rubbed her baby bump. That's what you thought too, right?

Yes, the woman murmured softly, her face turning pale. It had only been a loud noise, that was all. Then, she added: Just like that, a mundane life loses its mundanity. But her neighbor wasn't listening. She was busy stroking the child's cheek. And how are you today?

The woman stared blankly at this scene for a short while. Her neighbor began to play with the child. Rock, paper, scissors. The emergency bell stopped. Rock, paper, scissors. The alarm resounded in the woman's head, refusing to leave her. Rock, paper, scissors.

I'm sorry, the woman said. Her neighbor glanced up at her. Could you look after the child for me? Her neighbor stared at her in curiosity at this request. The woman averted her gaze. I want to do a little shopping. Of course, her neighbor answered. I love children, she added.

Be a good boy now, the woman said, placing a hand on the child's head. Yep, the child nodded. Come to auntie's house, the neighbor invited him. We've got a toy train you can play with.

The woman returned to her apartment alone, and stared at her face in the mirror. No one would be likely to guess just by looking at that face. That her life was free from hardship or want. She picked up a vial of perfume, a favorite of hers from before she had gotten married. And then she sprayed it on her neck.

Ever since I was a child, I wanted to be a writer. But not anymore. Now, I'm a housewife. Now, I realize full well that I'm not cut out to be a writer. I'm sure of it. I would exhaust all my ideas in a single work. I would end up writing about a woman whose life, both past and present, is just like mine. In a Japanese context, that would make it an I-novel, I suppose. But the genre doesn't matter. A novel featuring a woman just like me would appear on the bookstore shelves, and then someone would buy it. That reader would point to me and say: See, she's written a novel about herself. The only action available to me would be to remain silent. I wouldn't be able to affirm the charge, nor deny it.

That woman who looks like me, who might even *be* me, would live in an apartment complex somewhere far from the city center. She would live in this small apartment with her healthy and good husband, along with a young son who may or may not be destined to one day become a successful member of society. Her husband would be the factory manager at a bookbindery. Once a month, the three of them would go to a restaurant together on what they called a date. They would travel abroad once a year. Theirs wouldn't be an extravagant lifestyle, but the woman would be able to enjoy a life free from hardship or want.

There are always bloodstains when you wrap someone's body with bandages. The same can be said for this woman. They aren't anything special. There isn't anything special about my bloodstains, about my loneliness, about my past, about the injuries and harm done to me by the men in my past. So if I were to write a novel, the protagonist would be a woman like that.

Eventually, there comes a moment when the woman takes action. In other words, when the story begins. For her, it is a day like any other. Why that day? She doesn't have any special reason. Just like how those who commit suicide may have no clear reason for choosing that particular day. It simply happens that an insignificant trigger sets the chain of events in motion. The woman is preparing dinner with her child. The menu could be, well, anything. Preferably something as mundane as possible. Various noises echo throughout the evening apartment complex. Women's voices. The bugle of a door-to-door tofu merchant. A kitchen timer. A children's television program. These sounds distract the woman from her bloodstains, lull her into feeling as though they never existed.

Suddenly, a sound rings out, nailing the woman to the spot. It could be an alarm, a siren, something like that. When we hear such sounds, our first instinct is to do something, to take action. Then, after a few seconds of thought, we might think, for example, to run, to put out a fire, or to protect ourselves from an earthquake. This woman is no different. She is spurred to take action, but doesn't know how to act. A single image floats into her mind, but the sound of the child's voice drowns it out.

After a short while, the identity of that searing sound becomes clear. Silence falls again over the apartment complex. But the alarm in the woman's mind won't stop ringing. It urges her to act, quickly. The scene that a moment earlier had been drowned out from her head is born again.

She leaves the child with an acquaintance, and alone, packs her suitcase. Then, she departs. In the back of her mind, her thoughts are consumed by a mushroom cloud, slowly swaying, slowly expanding.

The reason why I can't make my bloodstains special is because I'm unable to think of any words that can describe them as special. Sometimes, I find myself thinking that if only I could depict myself in detail, like a novelist, with the skill to differentiate between my experiences and those of others, I might be able to do it. But just what form would it take? Even if I could write a book worthy of stirring people's emotions, something that might bring them to tears, that wouldn't change the fact that I'm still just an ordinary, mediocre person.

The woman looked down at the clouds from the airplane. A young couple was sitting in the row in front of her. Look, said the young woman, you can see the clouds down below. They're beautiful, the man replied. You can see lights from towns between the clouds. Overhearing this, the woman too stole a cautious, careful peek at the world below. She could make out spots of light beneath the clouds. A vision came to her, of a presence as pure as smoke wafting from dry ice, spreading through the city in concentric circles. The bomb had been dropped a long time ago. By the time that she had been born, even that tragedy had become no more than a memory, a memory to which the only response was to break down in tears. Every day, she did exactly those things that every housewife does. She applied herself to bleaching her husband's shirts, as though to affirm his masculine spirit. But even when faced with something to which the only natural response could be tears, the woman couldn't bring herself to cry. Not even loving her child had ever felt like an obligation. It wasn't that she *didn't* cry—she *couldn't*. Who could have known that there were horrors in this world that couldn't be healed through tears?

The Samaritan woman met Christ at the well, and heard about the living water there. "Whoever drinks of the water that I shall give him will never thirst; the water that I shall give him will become in him a spring of water welling up to eternal life." The Samaritan woman desired that water. "Sir, give me this water, that I may not thirst, nor come here to draw." The Samaritan woman thought of Christ's spiritual gift as drinking water from a well. A conversation between two passersby. Two coins of different value, both called *water*, exchanged between God and man. This unfair monetary exchange takes place between all people and the Evangelist. No one can know the meaning of the Gospel without the help of the Evangelist. Every person is that Samaritan woman. Every time they read the story of the Samaritan woman, they are reading a story in which they themselves appear. No one can be as symbolic as God. The Samaritan was a thirsty woman. Though married to five men, still she was unable to find satisfaction, and vacillated over becoming involved with a sixth. The Samaritan woman thought that she could quench her thirst with water from a well. No one can laugh at this woman.

My brother was an alcoholic. He ended his life too young. He had beautiful, intelligent eyes, and a habit that he was powerless to resist, of drinking from the early hours of the morning. It was clear that he wasn't in a rational state of mind when he drank, but I never knew the reason why. According to him, it was because he was bored. Probably not even he knew precisely why he craved alcohol so much. When he drank, his face would turn puffy, his eyes red. His gaze would grow sharper, more intense. But drinking was unable to cure him of that boredom, and he ended up trying to leap from the roof of our apartment building. Because of that, he spent a long stint in and out of hospital. He was prescribed so many antipsychotics that he couldn't take them orally, and would fall into a long sleep only when they were injected directly into his veins. For those brief moments, he was able to forget his boredom. Eventually, through long rehabilitation and counselling, he managed to overcome his alcoholism. Afterward, he diligently set out looking for a job, and found a part-time position as a telephone recruiter for a cram school company. There, he recruited an average of eight students each day, four times more than the typical recruiter. He leaped off the building the day that he was promoted to a full-time position. Our mother still thinks that he died in a rational state of mind.

I often find my thoughts turning to my brother. I loved him. To me, he was an ideal being. If man is the evolved form of ape, he was the evolved form of me. He drank. He killed himself. He died in a rational state of mind. God gave courage to my brother, and cowardice to me. What's wrong? someone called out to me. It was my future husband. Do you feel sick? I was in his apartment. No, I responded, it's nothing. I'll tidy up. The remnants of a home-cooked meal littered the table. We were playing house before we made our marriage official. It was reassuring to know that my brother and my future husband didn't resemble one another in the slightest. Every now and then, I remembered what my brother said: I'm bored. Bored to death. Early in the morning, while it was still dark outside, my brother used to knock on my bedroom door. I'm bored. Let's go play billiards, he would say. It's too early, I would answer him. The pool hall isn't open yet. You've been drinking again, haven't you?

I poured the leftover dressing down the sink, and started washing the dishes. I'll help, my future husband said, and began wiping them with a dry dishtowel. He hummed a song. He didn't drink much. He didn't find his surroundings boring. His mind was clear. He wasn't like my brother. I had no choice but to cling to this man, to be a parasite feeding off his sanity. I couldn't share in my brother's madness. If I did, I would die.

My future husband stroked my head. Don't be too hard on yourself, he said. You've got your whole life to get the hang of it, so there's no need to go overboard trying to cook up a feast right from the get-go. I rested my head against his shoulder. Maybe I *have* been pushing myself a little, I said. I don't want to put in any less than you, your effort, your perseverance. His tenacity, his strength. His honest gaze. Eyes unable to see the boredom that my brother knew only too well. He would make me a decent person too. He would drag me out from the sea of my brother in which I was floundering, pull me up onto a craggy rock, and order me to walk on my own two feet.

I held fast to him as I took him in my arms. His well-toned muscles embraced me. I could be dependent on him. If he could hold me in those strong arms of his, I could break free. I would rob him of that energy, drain him to the point of exhaustion. That was the kind of couple that we would be, I thought.

It was around nine o'clock in the evening when the woman checked into the hotel in Nagasaki. She looked over the pamphlet. The hotel was built and decorated in a Portuguese style, it read. The photos of the mosaic in the courtyard and the stained-glass windows by the stairs caught her eye. She had left her house as though in flight. Her nerves were on edge. She wouldn't be able to sleep for a while. The only option available to her was to wander around town until sleep bore down on her. She left her bulky suitcase at the front desk. I'm going for a walk, she said. Fierce thirst struck her. She asked if there was anywhere nearby where she could get a drink. The concierge at the front desk suggested a bar in a hotel by the shore, a converted ferry ship. It had a good view of the bay, he told her. For the first time since she had married her husband, the woman went to drink by herself.

My mother didn't approve of me drinking. She had been that way long before my brother died. My brother would steal money from our mother's purse to fuel his alcoholism. But our mother never said anything to him. Even when the doctors told her not to let him drink, she continued to tolerate his actions. And so, with the blessing of our mother's neglect, my brother could drink, could hurl himself from our rooftop, whenever he pleased. He could die whenever he pleased.

After my brother left this world, my mother began to inspect my wrists at every opportunity. She would gently slip her fingers under them as she pretended to greet me. That unnaturally thin smile of hers. It still arouses feelings of disgust in me. If I happened to have so much as a small scratch on me, she would let out an ear-rending scream. She would strip me naked, inspect every inch of my body. All to make sure that I wasn't edging toward death.

She allowed my brother to descend into madness, to take his own life, but not me. She ordered me to look up to him, now a star in the sky, while walking the balance beam of sanity alone. When I realized this, I knew that she didn't love me. She had only ever loved my brother. That's awful, Mom. My beloved mother. My brother would get drunk, and kiss her on the cheek. She would start to cry. I could never kiss her like that. Not even if I had wanted to. It was always my brother's job to make her cry. He was an angel of pure narcissism. And that angel monopolized our mother's affections.

The hotel bar was located on the bridge of the former ferry ship. The woman took a seat, and immediately ordered a glass each of beer and of vodka. The bartender startled at this request. She wanted both of them, she insisted. The bartender acquiesced. She used the beer as a chaser as she drank down her vodka. Yorsh. She had learned this way of drinking in the past. She didn't get to do it often. Not without a side of greasy foie gras. The bar didn't have many side dishes to choose from. Instead of foie gras, she ordered cheese. When she was younger, she used to think that she would shower herself in drink once she left her parents. Her husband, on the other hand, was kind natured. He didn't drink much himself, but he didn't stop her from doing so either. Nor did he call her a kitchen drinker, despite the fact that she often liked to steal a glass or two while preparing dinner. It was as though he knew that if he were to use that word, she would well and truly become an alcoholic. He was adept at managing her. The alcohol whirled around her empty stomach. A few more drinks, and she would be able to sleep. She couldn't allow herself to get excited. Succumbing to despair would be even worse.

One day, I was in particularly low spirits. So low that you could probably call it depression. My husband suggested that I have a drink. You always feel better when you've had something to drink, he said. I was surprised to hear him say that. My mother had always forbidden me alcohol as a means of lightening my mood. I rejected his suggestion. I'll give it a rest tonight, I said. I understood that it was dangerous to let myself feel too animated at times like this. My husband would never know the dazzling heights of my mood at such times. The dangerous charm of that brilliant glow. At such moments, I would feel as though I had become a cherub or a seraph. I would wonder whether there truly was such a thing as suffering in this world. My memories would become dull and muted. I would think to myself. If there was a time to die, it was now. No matter the height, it wouldn't hurt if I jumped. I couldn't believe that my brother had leaped to his death in a rational state of mind. Did my mother still entertain such ridiculous thoughts? My brother had freed himself from his alcoholism by his own efforts. He reentered society, found a full-time job, and won the praise of everyone around him. Sparkling pinpoints of beautiful light, like granules of course-grain sugar, enveloped him. He had been so blinded by that mysterious honor that he could no longer stand it.

The woman rarely drank yorsh, and so soon got drunk. The hotel where she was staying wasn't far, but she took a taxi back.

She retrieved her room key from the front desk. A youth—a foreigner, judging by his appearance—was signing in. The woman collected her suitcase. She barely managed to drag it along behind her. She waited for the elevator. The youth stood beside her. When the elevator arrived, the two stepped inside. The doors slid shut. The elevator began to ascend, leaving the woman feeling weightless.

Um, the youth called out, hesitating. Shall I help with your luggage? His Japanese was flawless—so perfect that it seemed almost comical coming from the lips of this topaz-eyed young man. Are you talking to me? the woman asked. Of course I am. There's no one else here, is there? The woman laughed at this. You're a bit of a quibbler, aren't you? The woman understood, intuitively, that she could be aggressive with this youth. Sorry, he apologized. As she had expected. Your Japanese is good, she commented. Yes, he nodded.

You offered to help with my luggage, didn't you? The woman stared at the youth seductively. Like a young girl. But she didn't have the forceful vigor of a young girl anymore. Yes, the youth replied happily. You look like you've had a lot to drink. I'm not drunk, the woman responded, almost falling backward. The youth grabbed her clothes to support her. The woman remembered her loneliness. The youth didn't so much as attempt to casually touch her body. In spite of her vulnerability, he somehow managed to virtuously hold onto her clothes, to help her regain her balance without so much as brushing up against her. He was such a cowardly and pure young man.

You *are* drunk. Let me take that. The youth seized her luggage. It seemed that while he wouldn't touch her body, he had no trouble snatching her suitcase. Thank you, she said highhandedly. As though acknowledging a bellboy. I went out to a bar, and had too much to drink. You never know your own limits when you're drinking by yourself. The woman smiled at him. The youth smiled back. Are you traveling alone? he asked. What about your family? Family. The woman understood that he didn't mean her parents. He was tacitly asking if she had left her husband and child behind somewhere. Do you want to know if I'm married? she teased. I'm sorry. I didn't mean to be rude. The youth hung his head. He held her suitcase in his arms. His muscles bulged under the heavy weight.

I *was* married, long ago. The woman leaned against the elevator wall. Five times, she said, emphasizing the number with her fingers. I've married five men, but none of them were ever able to satisfy me. Now I'm wondering whether I should try my luck with a sixth one. The woman laughed. The youth continued to stare at the floor, without answering. As though he had been terribly humiliated. The woman took satisfaction from his reaction. The elevator came to a stop. The woman extended her hand. Thank you. You can give me my suitcase now. But the youth didn't hand it back to her. The woman walked backward out of the elevator. My suitcase, please. The youth stepped out as well. The doors slid shut. The elevator continued climbing upward. Give it to me.

This is a heartbreak trip, isn't it? You're trying to overcome your grief, right? the youth murmured. I don't know the details though. How rude, the woman responded. Fancy saying that to someone you've just met. I'm sightseeing, that's all. You must be a hollow, lonely little man to make a pathetic joke like that.

I feel sorry for you. The youth reached out to touch the woman. She pushed him away, hitting him with an open-handed slap. The youth raised his hand to his cheek, staring down at the floor. His was the face of a wounded heart. The face of a victim. The woman was shocked to see something so miserable, so wretched.

I'm sorry I hit you, the woman murmured, her voice quivering. I know you mean well, she said once she managed to calm herself. You may be right about this being a heartbreak trip. I'll admit that. So please, forgive me. I was taken aback, hearing a stranger say he feels sorry for me.

The youth shed tears. I should have said I love you. Not that I feel sorry for you. If I had, maybe you wouldn't have hit me. I'll keep my distance from now on. That would be best. I never know what to do when people get angry at me.

The woman fell silent. The youth was observing her, closely. With those pure, fragile eyes of his. Because he felt a subconscious longing for her. Before she knew it, the woman had seduced this man by invoking his sense of sympathy. I feel better now that I've seen you cry, she said. You can come to my room, if I haven't annoyed you enough already.

The youth followed behind her.

No sooner did the woman enter the room than she fell exhausted onto the bed. The youth placed her luggage on the sofa. I need water, the woman said. Can you bring me a bottle from the fridge? The rooms here don't have fridges. You can take mine, if you want. The youth retrieved a plastic bottle from his bag. Thank you. I'm so thirsty. The woman gulped down the water. Beads of moisture ran down her neck. The youth laughed, offering her a handkerchief. When you get older, you forget how much drink you can hold, the woman said. The youth nodded. He sat down on the sofa a short distance away from her, beside her luggage. There's a saying about that, the youth said. If you don't know your limits, you can end up stopping yourself too soon. The woman laughed. People must drink a lot where you come from, she said. Anyway, are foreigners these days skipping Kyoto for Nagasaki?

I'm Japanese, the youth answered. My mother was born overseas, if you're wondering about my appearance, but *I* was born here in Japan. Ah, I see, the woman nodded. They do say that the fresh, clean skin of mixed-race Japanese is the most beautiful. The woman rose to her feet, and stared at the texture of the skin around his neck and shoulders. My skin isn't beautiful. The youth looked away. There's nothing interesting about me. I want to know more about *you*. What are you doing in Nagasaki all by yourself?

Me? You want to know about *me*? The woman stared into the distance. She delved deep into her heart. She never spoke much about herself. If she were to lie to this youth, or try to deceive him, he would no doubt see straight through her. And he would be hurt by it. The woman was used to being hurt, but not to hurting others. Doing something like that would require considerable strength.

She let out a weary sigh.

The reason why she had come to this distant land. If she were to try to put it in words, she sensed, she would merely end up describing the mundanity of everyday life. Things related to everyday life, things that needed saying. But if she were to relate all that, it would sound like nothing more than a playful joke. Even if she tried to tell him, he would no doubt realize that it would be no different from her saying nothing all.

The youth didn't have the power to trespass into her mind. But he hated talking about himself more. This youth, this young man with no capacity to do wrong, hated himself.

This is my life these days. As much as I said I need to talk, there's really nothing to say. When I'm short on money, I cook silver salmon. When I'm well off, I make beef stew. Food shouldn't be all there is to living. But that's what I would end up talking about. So basically, there isn't a lot that happens in my life.

What about your past? the youth asked. I said I felt sorry for you. But that feeling came to me subconsciously. I want to know why.

There are all kinds of people, with all kinds of pasts. I know that. Women whose fathers beat them, who still bear the scars to this day. Women who fall in love with married men. Women who starve themselves because they're afraid to eat. But when it comes to me. . . Ah, I don't have anything. Only an incident, a major incident, but one that happened so long ago I can't even remember. That's all. I don't even remember what it was. And that doesn't make for a good story. It's like a burn scar that I've been carrying with me, but that isn't enough to talk about.

But you came to Nagasaki, the youth said.

That's right. It only surfaced at that moment, the woman answered. There was a loud noise. It was. . .an emergency bell, yes. That's when it struck me. The mushroom cloud. I've felt like that ever since I first saw it. I'm obsessed with that mushroom cloud, that's all. One sunny day, a cloud as pure as a white wedding dress appeared overhead. A fantastic shape. Who would have thought it could kill so many? I live in an apartment complex, in a small flat divided into still smaller rooms. A child's festering back, a twisted, melted soft-drink bottle. That's the kind of small, worthless world I inhabit. But when the emergency bell went off, all I could think about was that mushroom cloud.

After saying this, the woman touched the youth's hand. Why don't you sit next to me? She wanted to destroy the youth's virtue. She spoke in a sweet voice. So sweet that she herself found it sickening.

We can't. The youth pulled his hand away. I don't want to get rejected again because I let myself get too close to you.

A long time ago. . . the woman murmured after a pause. She let out a heavy sigh. A long time ago, someone I loved gave up their life. I was so captivated by his action that I thought about dying too, but my parents wouldn't let me.

I'd feel the same way if you died. I mean, I'd feel drawn in. I might die as well.

The two pressed their lips together. If she violated the

prohibition against infidelity, perhaps she could escape the prohibition of death, the woman thought.

The youth hesitated as she began to undress him.

He looked suddenly frightened, and began to claw at his arms.

In the end, the woman tired without the act proceeding to its ultimate conclusion. The reason was probably more fundamental than the youth's skin condition, his atopy. His naked embrace and his horribly tormented personality were enough by themselves to satisfy her desire. The youth didn't seem to share the common goal of most men, the insertion of the penis, and so no sooner did he make sure that she was satisfied than he went to take a shower. Then, no doubt remembering that she had said that she was thirsty, he bought a beer from the vending machine in the corridor outside.

Are you okay with more alcohol? The youth handed her the beer. It's fine. I can drink, the woman answered as she accepted it. I had some water earlier, so I've sobered up now. The two of them drank in bed.

Your face looks terrible. Wounded. The woman stared into the youth's eyes. They seemed to be crying out that she had violated him against his will. No, the youth said. I was just surprised. I've never had a woman make love to me like that before.

It just made me think all of a sudden, the youth murmured. About why you came to this land. Once I started thinking about it, I even forgot about my own sense of inferiority.

The youth raised his hand to the woman's cheek. You came here in search of water, to quench your thirst.

Everyone was thirsty that day, the woman answered. It was already summer, the hottest day of the year. The temperature reached six thousand degrees. Everyone was searching for water. How are you supposed to know the feelings of all the people who find themselves in a place like that? You said I was thirsty, but what could my thirst possibly have in common with theirs?

You should go to Urakami tomorrow, the youth said. Urakami? Urakami Cathedral? the woman asked. Not only there. The Peace Park and the Atomic Bomb Museum aren't far from the cathedral. You might realize something if you go there. Something you don't know yet. I don't know the answer, so it would probably be best for you to go there and learn it for yourself.

You're a funny one, aren't you? The woman laughed. You'll just watch on from the sidelines while I solve this mystery by myself. You're so helpless.

I *am* helpless, the youth murmured.

I'll go to Urakami. Alone. We can just eat together and sleep together, Mr. Helpless.

Let's do it like that. Whatever you want, we can do it like that. I don't want to be a nuisance. So I won't go with you.

That's right. You're a nuisance. The woman laughed. You're so servile. You won't even tell me anything about yourself. I've never met a man like you before. Every man I've ever known has always made himself out to be either lucky or unlucky. Or both. They think they can become the richest man in the world if their job works out, and if it doesn't, they'll ask me to commit suicide with them. But you're different.

In that case, if I tell you about myself, can I make you mine?

Yes. That's the only kind of man I've ever known.

I don't have anything to say though.

Why not?

Why should I need to tell my story to a woman who came to this land trying to quench the thirst of six thousand degrees? No story of mine can compare to that thirst. All I can do is weep. You don't believe in love, do you? For you, love is like a shadow seared into stone by a brilliant flash of light.

I could be anyone's woman, the woman said. You can do it the same way as every other man I've known. Just talk about yourself, tell me my own story is vulgar, call me ugly. You should seize me and violate me, just like any other man would, just like everyone else has up till now. I won't resist.

The youth cried. Just as the woman didn't know love, so too did it seem that he didn't know how to love a woman, or even how to make a woman whom he didn't love his own.

Morning. The woman and the youth ate breakfast together in the hotel restaurant. The woman interrogated the youth about himself. How old are you? Where do you live? What's your name? She knew that it was painful for him to answer such questions. She had taken a liking to his unidentified pain. I want to know everything about you, she said. As much as possible. The youth's atopy looked to have flared up from stress. He scratched his arm as he began to recount his story, as though responding to an inquisition.

The youth's mother was born and raised in Moscow. When she was twenty-six years old, she met a Japanese man, an interpreter, and returned with him to his home country. At that time, she had been a citizen of the Soviet Union, acquiring Japanese citizenship shortly before the collapse of the Eastern Bloc. The youth was born in Japan.

Based on your age, you must be a university student, the woman said. That's right, the youth nodded. I just graduated. This is my graduation trip.

She asked the youth his Japanese name. It was an exceptionally mundane name. Next, she asked what people called him in Russian. He tried to hide this one. I don't like my name, he said.

I'm named after a saint. A famously strong one. According to legend, he practiced asceticism in a forest for fifteen years, and even tamed a bear there. Ever since I was little, my mother would tell me the story of that saint whenever I cried, so I always wished that his name wasn't mine.

You know a lot about your patron saint, don't you? The woman stared at the crucifix pinned to the youth's jacket. She could recognize the denomination to which he belonged from the shape of that cross. I know your saint, she said. I know your name. If you're still a fervent churchgoer, then you belong to. . .

Pravoslavie, the youth answered. Yes, the woman murmured. That's what you call it in Russian, isn't it? You're Japanese, yet the color of those eyes. . . Then there's your pin. And you use words that only Russians use. But your Japanese is excellent. And you sleep with Japanese women.

Is there something wrong with that? The youth stared down at the table. Am I not allowed to sleep with Japanese women? Because I'm of mixed blood?

No. The woman stared at the youth's face. That doesn't matter. But you looked humiliated while I was holding you. Your expression made it seem like it wasn't consensual. And even now your eyes look pained.

I must have hurt your feelings, no? It was consensual. If I tell you it was consensual, can you forgive me? How much do you long for it, I wonder? A man inserting his member inside of you, the satisfaction of having completed that act. The satisfaction of having gained something. Like shooting a hare with a gun. Because it's a contradictory desire, wanting to find that kind of man, without even caring if his performance is all just one big lie. Wanting to see a man who can play that role, who can be satisfied just by the insertion of the phallus.

Are you asking if that's what I want? If that's how I want to see you? Because I don't know. But I've only ever known men like that before. That's all. I don't know whether it's what I want. And I don't have the faintest clue whether it's what I *should* want.

The woman remembered. The men who dug into her vagina. With their fingers, with their penises. The faces of all those men blurred together. When the act was over, a pallid expression would always fall over the woman's face. It wasn't intentional. Her face would harden like stone. She couldn't even fake a smile. When that happened, the men, confused, would ask her what was wrong. They would tilt their heads to one side in obvious displeasure. She couldn't offer them any words of explanation. She couldn't even feel any sense of disgust toward them. After the act of intercourse was finished, the woman's heart was a thirsty well. Without feeling, there were no words. Her husband was better than the other men whom she had known, maybe. He apologized. As though he thought that he had been rough with her. He was a good man. He wasn't vastly different from the others, but even if only a little, he always performed the act with affection for her.

But this mixed-race youth was clearly different from the other men whom she had known. Different from her husband too. He was meager and unimposing, and there was something pathetic about him, the woman thought. She had always believed that men would hurt her, but he was different. This youth was himself fragile, unable to hurt another. Even her good-natured husband had hurt her. His simple belief that the act was genuine filled her with anxiety. Her pure and righteous husband would never forgive her repulsive despair, she thought.

After parting ways with the youth at the restaurant, the woman headed toward Urakami. It didn't seem to be particularly far from the hotel, so she took a taxi. *Pravoslavie*, the woman recited. Eastern Orthodoxy. That was how it was known in Japan. The woman reminisced on a time now passed. She had once attended an Orthodox church herself. The Holy Resurrection Cathedral in Tokyo's Surugadai district. She had never been baptized.

*

It was the night before Pentecost when I first visited the Tokyo Holy Resurrection Cathedral. I simply sat there in a daze, watching the ritual being carried out. At one point, I was told to line up.

The priest drew a cross on the foreheads of all those present with an oiled brush. He drew one on my forehead too. When I wiped the oil off my eyelids, I smelled a strange fragrance. After that, I came back to the church often, whenever I felt like it.

Eventually, my mother realized where I was going. Whenever I tried to go back, she would try every trick that came to mind to stop me. Tidy your room, she might say. Finish your homework. Once, she even suggested, completely out of the blue, that we go skiing. Her efforts became more and more overt. One Sunday morning, she even went so far as to lock me in my upstairs bedroom. I slipped on the pair of sandals left out on the balcony, and leaped to the ground. When I came home, I learned that she had called the police. They treated me as a burglar who had escaped from the balcony. It was as though my flight had been a crime, while my mother's confinement of me had been completely justified. She said that she would forgive me. From that day on, I stopped going to church.

The Bible doesn't indicate why the Samaritan woman had relations with six men. Was it a physical thirst? A spiritual one? We don't even know who those six men were. Would we have a different opinion of the Samaritan woman if we knew more about those men, about their personalities and characters? If all six were arrogant, we might see her as pitiful. If they were all young and attractive, she might be considered lascivious. But the six men are like cold objets d'art, deprived of all identity. Sometimes, I think of the men who have passed me by as these six men bound by anonymity. Each of them puffed with arrogance when he believed that he was loved. Each of them acted like a fawning youth when he desired more. I don't know if they themselves were to blame for why I hated them so much.

I've never enjoyed going out with men. When I go to a holiday resort with a man, it feels like my whole body has been taken over by frostbite. Alone in the crowd, I start to feel depressed, as though my arm linked with his has turned rotten and numb. His whispered words of love turn into hollow symbols, unable to resonate with me. When my luck runs thin, he will be too busy enjoying himself. When my luck flows thick, he might act all worried. At such times, a man's attitude can change from good to bad on nothing more than a whim. It isn't a worthy means of judging his character. Sometimes, I might feel unwell when we reach our destination, and ask to stop at a café to rest—anywhere would be fine. But some men would insist that they want alcohol, and would drag me across town until they found a bar that caught their interest. Nonetheless, such episodes never led to a fight or a breakup. A kinder man would probably have called a taxi and let me rest back at the hotel. A more sensitive man would have offered to take me home if I wasn't enjoying myself. But is there really any difference between these men? If I don't like being around men, it doesn't matter how nice they are. Frightened by the crowds at the holiday resort, I would grab the man's arm. I had nowhere else to turn. Some men would misunderstand that gesture and feel pleased with themselves. Others would ask me worriedly how I was feeling. To me, they were both the same. I couldn't explain my situation either way.

Every time I go somewhere with a man, I find myself plagued with confusion. A stream of incoherent symbols floods my mind, my body overloading with sensations that I can't put into words. Back when I would mistakenly attribute that feeling to disgust for the man in question, I would break up with him. But ever since I realized that those men didn't lie at the heart of how I felt, I started going out with anyone who invited me, no matter how awful they were. I always tried to pull myself out of that state, to talk to them. And I always found myself burning with frustration when I couldn't do it.

The glass door slid open without a hitch. That was only natural, the woman realized. They were automatic doors. She glanced around the main entrance. The building was immaculate, and looked to have been designed with considerable attention to architectural aesthetics. It reminded her of a hospital. Whiteness and curves. She wondered whether people associated such things with peace.

She found the entrance at the bottom of a spiraling slope. There, she bought a ticket, and made her way to the automatic entrance gate. The room beyond was shrouded in darkness. The woman hesitated. It wasn't like the museum in Hiroshima. The Hiroshima Peace Memorial Museum displayed various objects in glass cases arranged in brightly lit rooms, things like clothes worn by survivors of the atomic bombing. The Nagasaki Atomic Bomb Museum, however, felt almost like entering a choreographed stage production.

She stepped gingerly through the automatic ticket gates. It was dark inside. She could hear the loud sound of a clock ticking. Uneasiness fell over her. A clock in an illuminated display. It was broken. The hands pointed to 11:02, the minute that the atomic bomb was dropped. That alone was enough to explain its significance. The exaggerated sound of the ticking clock. Fear took hold of the woman. She escaped to the next room.

The space was dimly lit, as though by an old miniature light bulb. Photographs of the city of Nagasaki and Urakami Cathedral in the immediate aftermath of the attack. Lots of digital monitors. Dead bodies appeared on the screens, testimonies and diary entries from that day. She could still hear the ticking of the clock. The woman's anxiety didn't abate. A statue of Christ rose up in front of her. She was afraid. She suspected that she might be killed by that statue. It didn't occur to her that the atomic bomb would kill her.

The woman was struck with relief when she entered a normal room free from those special effects. She looked over a model of the city of Nagasaki. It was well made. As she approached the model, a recording began to play. The city of Nagasaki, August 9, 1945. Population: two hundred and forty thousand. Number of deaths caused by the blast: seventy-three thousand eight hundred and eighty-four. Number of injured: seventy-four thousand nine hundred and nine. No sooner did the voice read the numbers out than it disappeared. The model lit up in concentric circles. Those circles, representing the damage caused by varying degrees of radiation, spread across the city. The woman was fascinated by them, so beautiful and precise.

Glancing around the room, the woman caught sight of a number of children dressed in school uniforms. One of them was hugging a full-size model of the Fat Man bomb. Hey, this thing's cold, he said. It's nice and cool.

In the glass cases by the walls were a photograph of a woman's burned back, a steel helmet with pieces of a skull stuck to it, and other displays. It was the same as what she had seen in Hiroshima. There was a melted soft-drink bottle next to a placard indicating that visitors were free to touch it. The glass was twisted and distorted. It was cold to the touch. The temperature that glass is meant to be. Nice and cool. She realized that she was sharing the same impression as the child hugging the Fat Man replica a moment ago. It was cold. At this point in time, that was. In any event, this point in time was all that the woman could understand. She was hungry. She glanced at her watch. It was almost noon.

A champon noodle restaurant. The woman remembered her husband. Her husband often took her to restaurants. He would call it a date. She would be expecting an unpretentious local eatery, maybe one of those in front of the station, but he would take her instead to a high-class restaurant. She could only wonder how he had found it. He wanted to make her feel comfortable, to take her somewhere fancy for a change of scenery. He was a kind, considerate person. The woman was tempted to tell him that they didn't need to go to all the trouble of eating out. At that moment, she remembered the words of the only man whom she had ever loved. You look like a prisoner. I am too. I'm going to escape from this prison life someday. But as for the woman, she went on dates as much as possible. As though to make sure that no one could ever tell her that she looked like a prisoner again. She ate French cuisine in an atmospheric restaurant. A toast with champagne. She took her knife to her plate of roast duck without uttering so much as a word. Her husband spoke about his work and friends. The woman nodded along. She didn't have anything in particular to talk about. It wasn't as though he was the kind of man who didn't listen to her. Her husband was an attentive listener. Housework, childcare, the neighbors. Nor was it as though nothing ever changed, or no new topics ever came up. If anything, it was simply that she didn't have any desire to communicate such things. Housework, childcare, or getting to know the neighbors. Even if a man were to make fun of her for such things, she wouldn't get angry, her heart wouldn't be wounded. As though she had long since braced herself against his reaction. The woman carried out that work as though to atone for her sins. If that person were still alive, would he still say that hers was the face of a prisoner? If these dates were supposed to be a reward for all her hard work, she didn't need them. She had married this good-natured man and borne his child, but still she felt no desire to chew greedily on happiness. The roast duck that her husband had given her practically as a gift rested on her tongue. She didn't try to chew it. She didn't try to taste it. She swallowed it down in secret, leaving behind only suffering. There was no need to reward such a sinful woman as her.

The woman returned to the hotel shortly after noon. She made her way to the youth's room. She rang the doorbell. The youth didn't answer. The woman sighed. At this time of day, most tourists would be out exploring the city. She should have known better, she thought with a sigh.

Just as she lifted her finger from the doorbell, the youth appeared. What's the matter? he asked. I should be asking you that. Aren't you going out today? the woman responded without answering his question.

I went to the Glover Residence this morning, the youth replied. I'm writing a postcard to a friend. They were selling a lot of nice postcards there.

Do you want to come in? The youth laughed. Let me show you all the postcards I bought. He invited the woman into his room.

Here they are. The youth motioned for her to sit on the bed. She flipped through the stack. I'll make some tea, the youth said. One of the postcards has a beautiful nighttime view. That's my favorite. I decided to keep it for myself. The youth handed the woman a teacup. Be careful. It's hot.

The woman put the postcards on the bed, and took the teacup in both hands. She stared into the distance. Vaguely. Without saying anything.

Did something happen? The youth sat down beside her.

You're very generous, letting me into your room.

Do you think so? I mean, *you* came to *me*. And I'm sure you would let me into your room too.

But you invited me in before I could even ask. Before I could even beg. Please, come inside, you said.

What's wrong with that?

There nothing *wrong* with it. No, it's just. . . It's the wrong way around. You're, well, sweet, and stupid.

I asked because I wanted to. I wanted you to come in. I thought it would be nice to show you all these postcards I bought. Because I like you.

If that's true, if you really do like me, isn't that all the more reason to hold the door shut? I would plead with you. Please, let me in. Please, I love you. You could pretend not to notice me ringing the doorbell, you could pretend not to notice how much I want to be let inside, you could ignore my begging. That's the kind of cruel game that men like to play, isn't it? Once you've had a woman, after that, it's all fun and games, right?

Fun and games. . . Sure, normal men might do that. But it wouldn't occur to me. I've always been like this. Like I was born with a disability, or something.

Me too. You called it an inferiority complex, that disability of yours. I just sit idly by and watch men play. I just watch them as they work themselves up. Before I knew it, I realized I was different from other women. . . You and me, we'll never be able to love anyone.

The youth's head drooped. I'm lonely, he said. I've never felt this alone before.

I'm lonely, the woman said. Some people might be able to face loneliness directly, but others can't.

That's true.

When you met me, that was the first time you ever looked directly on it, that loneliness that you had never felt before. Or rather, you stared into it for the first time.

You're right, the youth said. You're right about everything.

The two stared into each other.

Your face is so pale. Are all mixed-race people this color?

I don't know. In Russia, they say I have yellow skin. In Japan, people say I'm white. Even I wonder what color my face is.

You don't know anything about yourself, do you?

No.

You won't even make up your own mind.

I can't.

All you need to do is find someone, someone who knows how to make those decisions for you. And then you can obey them.

I want to obey you.

That won't do.

The woman hugged the youth. She kissed his neck. She traced the faint impressions that she left there with her fingers. She urged him to take off his clothes. He fumbled as he unbuttoned his shirt. He was like a girl about to have sex for the first time, still unfamiliar with love. Perhaps he was unable to accept the idea of sleeping with the woman while she still denied him affection.

I went there. To Urakami.

The woman pressed herself against the youth's chest, slowly pushing him down onto the bed.

I saw what Nagasaki looked like that day, recreated by the Japanese.

The woman pressed her lips against the youth's chest. They're cold, he said. The two of them stared into each other's eyes.

It was Nagasaki, exactly as the Japanese saw it.

The two pressed their lips together.

They're cold. Your body is cold too.

The youth pulled the woman close.

It's the air-conditioning. That's why spring is so cold in Nagasaki.

I heard it was already hot and humid that day, before it was dropped.

It was so cold in the museum too. I felt a chill, but I don't know whether it was because I was scared, or because of the air-conditioning.

Did you see the people with all those burns?

I saw a woman's festering back. But it wasn't only people who were burned. There were six soft drink bottles melted into one. An ivory seal that had swelled up like someone's big toe. There were so many things that represented heat. I saw them all. One after the other. I could feel my head becoming more and more inorganic. My flesh turned cold. I couldn't even visualize heat anymore.

But you said you came to this land to witness the thirst of six thousand degrees for yourself. Maybe here, you thought, you could lay eyes on that invisible thirst.

That's right. I wonder if my heart is festering like that woman's back. I wonder if the contours that define me have melted away like those of the soft drink bottles. I wonder if I've been warped like that ivory seal. I don't know. Sympathy? Because those things turned my heart cold and white. They swept away everything that my heart tried to compare them to.

What did you see in the museum?

I saw a tragic story, a story that rejected my whole existence. The Japanese describe that day so tragically, you know?

It *was* tragic. They're only describing it faithfully.

It's such a strange feeling. My mind was filled with tragedy when I came to Nagasaki, and other things too. But when I stood in the museum, I forgot all about them. That place has the power to render you unconscious. So I couldn't remember what else I had been thinking about, apart from tragedy.

If not tragedy, then sorrow, maybe? Or madness? Those too can be like an atomic bomb.

Sorrow? I wonder. I wonder if I've ever felt true sorrow.

And I don't remember ever going mad. Only the person I loved was mad.

Neither sorrow nor madness. Are you sure?

I am. I can't even remember crying, not since I was a girl.

Me neither.

The woman laughed. You're lying.

It's true. When I see someone else crying, or sunken into madness, I'm drawn in. Entranced. I start to lose track of what makes us different. Eventually, they die. And it's as if my soul has been torn out of me. As if my heart has died and only my body lives on.

We're similar, the two of us. That's what you're trying to say, isn't it? We think the same things. You feel sorry for me. Acutely.

We *are* similar. But I wonder if that's really the right word for us? You and me, we can be like anyone. It's always the other person who decides who we are. We don't have the power to resist, even if resisting would be what's best for them too.

The woman stroked the youth's back with her hand. Hey. You know what? she began. You know what? I haven't had many men say they love me. They're all the same. They say they're interested in me. They say they realized it a while back. But whenever I hear those words, everything goes so hazy, so terribly hazy. Are they laced with poison, those words? Or sweet honey? Either way, they always dull my thoughts.

But you seduce those men so wantonly, so blatantly. They're so quick to invite you to dinner.

That's true. Dinner. The story of a man and a woman always begins with a meal. Appetite. That's right. It begins with that fulfilment of desire. Let's go to a restaurant, the most expensive one around, the man says. Because you like that sort of thing. But I don't know. *Do* I like that sort of thing? Whenever I need to hand down that kind of judgment, it feels like I have a fishbone stuck in my throat. But I swallow it down. And I thank him for inviting me to that fancy restaurant. I take his arm, and I tell him how much I want to eat that fancy food, how grateful I am to be able to eat it. And then he says to me: You're a shameless, obscene woman.

Something must stick in your mind at such times. A doubt. But the contours of the question blur. And you take the man's words for granted. You're the one who linked arms with him, so you take it in your stride, whether he calls you shameless or obscene. You affirm it.

I don't know. I might be the one who takes his arm, but it's like I'm being forced to. That's how it feels. So what compels me to do it? Is it the man? Is it the people around me, the environment that shaped me into a woman? I don't know. I don't want to take his arm. He makes me feel sick. He isn't young, that's for certain. He has a rounded belly, greasy hair, dark circles under his eyes like bruised bananas.

But when you look at his face, you stop realizing how disgusting you thought he was, don't you? Like you anesthetized your gums and pulled out your own molars.

I anesthetized my own gums. You're right. You're absolutely right. My arm, linked with his, goes numb. At some point, I come back to my senses, and try to pull it away. But I can't. It's stuck beneath his sweaty armpit, like it's entangled in a wire puzzle, and I can't pull it out.

Then he drags you to a fancy restaurant. But the man has no idea he's dragging you.

Exactly. He'll take me to an Italian restaurant where they use lots of olive oil. And I'll imagine that it's olive oil that's coating his hair.

You drink the expensive wine the waiter recommends to you. You drink French wine in an Italian restaurant. The man will only drink French wine. Anything else won't be to his taste, he says.

Exactly. That's right. I want to escape that reality, I want to get away from that man, so I gulp down the wine, as much as I can. But I don't realize why I want to drink. And the man is happy just to watch me. Because he's booked a hotel room. He's happy to see that I'm a convenient, unscrupulous woman. But he doesn't forget to remind me how expensive the wine is. He tells me to savor the flavor. But that doesn't stop me from gulping it down.

The man all but devours the salmone marinato, the prosciutto, the pizza margherita, the spaghetti alla pescatora, doesn't he? You continue to drink as you watch him. Because you're disgusted by the sight.

That's right. The man's thick lips are sticky with olive oil. He doesn't wipe it off with a napkin. He just runs his tongue over his lips. Then he sips at the wine that he boasted so much about, and washes the basil off his teeth. He's already drunk. His oily hair is in disarray. Then he says: I watched you when you went to the bathroom just before. I thought you had a delicate body, but I was wrong. Your thighs are so burly. And then he says: But you're pretty now. You weren't beautiful at all when I first met you. Your only flaw now is that unusually defined collarbone of yours.

That's when you come back to your senses. But it's too late. You're overwhelmed by the man's ugliness. You can't move.

You're right, about everything. That's why I choose to suffer, to slip into a state of suspended animation. I pour myself a strong tranquilizer of wine, and wait for amnesia to kick in. The man laughs. I had no idea you had so many worries that you had taken to drugs, he says. He, he who calls himself a great fan of Nietzsche, says that.

I understand. I understand everything. There's no need to say anymore.

The youth stroked the woman's hair.

Close your eyes. Pretend to be one more corpse belonging to this land.

The woman slept.

When I close my eyes, I sink into darkness, a distant memory of degradation. People suffer degradation both physically and mentally. The presence or absence of the phallus transcends the biological realm. A sorrowful individual finds in themselves the most abstract of holes, a vagina, a darkness, and finds in others an equally abstract phallus. Some people see the phallus in the mother. The Great Mother, the Perfect, the Hermaphrodite. One can't escape the images that have gripped them since the womb. Fear and longing. They love only the mother. They live as whores who have made vows with their mothers. Eventually, they go mad with hunger for love. I've seen it happen to so many. They continue to worship their mothers, all the while saying that their mothers don't love them back. They spout that kind of confused nonsense, until for one brief moment, as though struck by piercing wisdom, they speak with utmost clarity.

I was still young when I first realized that I was my mother's whore. As I grew older, my sense of impending crisis grew stronger. I knew that at this rate, I would go mad. And so I searched for a great act of labor to throw off the onset of that madness.

Once, my brother holed himself up his room for days, until my mother, worried, ordered me to look in on him. I knocked on his door, but there was no response. Mom's worried about you, I called out. She says you haven't come out in days. Are you listening? Mom says we can go to the beach if you're not feeling well. What do you think? Are you listening? I'm coming in. There was no response. I encroached inside.

My brother was sitting naked on the floor, surrounded by a huge pile of empty beer cans. A solitary tear rolled down his cheek. I called out his name as I approached. But I couldn't touch him. To me, my brother's tears were something to be treasured.

How are you feeling? I asked. He shook his head, wiping away the tear. Did something happen with your girlfriend? I asked. At the time, my brother had been dating a certain girl.

I broke up with her, he answered. Every time I go out with her, I get all dizzy, and it's like. . . Ah! It's like a seizure. My brother sobbed. There you go again, I said. This wasn't the first time that my brother had broken up with a woman because of his *illness*. But I. . . My body. . . I wasn't thinking straight, and I. . . Don't tell anyone! he cried out. That's normal for someone your age, I said. I won't tell anyone. But if anyone *did* find out, they wouldn't blame you. Nonetheless, he beseeched me not to tell anyone, ever. Not his friends, not our mother. He said that he would die of embarrassment if anyone were to ever find out.

My brother covered his face with his hands. The whorl of his hair swirled chaotically behind his head, spinning like the Andromeda Galaxy. A deep cavity spread out before me. I was staring on countless stars. At times, the stars were nothing more than a collection of disordered dots. At others, those dots joined to form constellations. The veins and arteries flowing through me, the chaos of the dots and the order of the constellations, set my heart in motion, making it beat in rhythm. But in the confusion of the universe, what exactly determines the flow of one's arteries and veins is nothing more than chance, a roll of the dice. It was for this reason that I tried at times to put the anguish felt by my brother and me into words, and on other occasions, I gave up. The movements themselves were erratic, and I lived by an irregular heartbeat. This irregular heartbeat deprived me not only of the ability to try to express myself, but also of my motivation to live. I was forced to live suffocated by this irregular heartbeat. How could I live without knowing when the arteries of order, the blood of meaning, would flow into my heart once again?

But more grotesque still was the possibility that the women who kissed my brother and set the whorl of his hair into disarray, who stirred up that deep chaos, would reappear. There were whorls of confusion on the backs of their heads too. But they would devour my brother's body without even becoming aware of that confusion. Those arteries and veins would continue to move, and those women would live oblivious to their irregularities.

The woman slowly opened her eyes in the youth's embrace. The youth looked at her, and smiled. You slept well, he said, placing a hand on her head. What time is it? the woman asked. Seven o'clock, the youth answered. I'm hungry. The woman flashed him a pained smile. Shall we have dinner, like we planned? She stared across at him, tilting her head to one side.

You want to eat with me? The youth's expression was one of stern doubt. That's what I thought, the woman answered. You don't have any other plans? No, I'm fine. But are *you* really fine eating with *me*? the youth asked again. The woman became uneasy. Why? I thought that was what we promised. Are *you* bothered by *my* company?

No, the youth laughed. His expression was one of relief. I'm just a little surprised, that's all. If you're really okay with me, we should go now. Before you change your mind.

They hailed a taxi, and made their way to Dejima Wharf. Without meeting one another's gaze, they stared out the windows in opposite directions. They may have devoured each other's flesh, but they didn't hold hands or brush up against one another playfully. Because they weren't lovers. The intersection of their lives was only here in Nagasaki, only now, for this one brief instant.

The two walked along the deck by the shore for a few meters. They found a Spanish restaurant, and entered with unspoken agreement. The youth ordered a beer, and the woman a Kir. When the drinks arrived at the table, they drained them both at once. The two burst into laughter.

You don't drink much, do you? the woman asked.

That's right. How did you know?

Just a feeling.

A foghorn sounded out on the water.

Just a feeling.

I can't hear you. Can you say that again?

Just. A. Feeling.

Just a. . .

Right. Just a feeling, I said.

But you, you rely on alcohol.

That's right. I can't live without it.

You can live without men, but not alcohol.

Yes, I don't rely on men. . . You say that like you aren't a man yourself.

If you're going to live dependent on alcohol or another human being, I'm out of the question. . . This meat is hard to chew, don't you think?

It's certainly tough. I wonder what it is? It looks like some sort of barbecue. I don't remember ordering anything like this.

Let's take a look at the menu. . . There are pictures. . . Brochetas—Spanish-style skewers. Maybe this is it?

This kind of thing happens all the time. There's a disconnect between image and reality.

Are we talking about brochetas? Or something more abstract?

Both. You're a strange man.

Strange? Do you like strange men?

I neither like nor dislike them.

When I'm with you, I feel terribly passionate. I love you. I'm sure of it.

The woman fell silent.

Do you remember my skin?

Your atopy, you mean?

My atopy. . . Not just that. How pale it is. Because I'm mixed-race. Or anything, really. I've got insect bites on my shoulder too.

The hours run away from me when I look at your skin. That's how I pass the time in this land.

The two kissed. Intensely. Indecently. They ruffled each other's hair, so much so that the whorls of their hair disappeared, their tongues clearly overlapping through their wide-open lips, pressed hard against each other. A lady walking past them with her dog startled. The bartender shook a cocktail, pretending not to have noticed. The waiter placed a bowl of zucchini gratin in front of them.

You're just killing time? the youth asked between quick, light kisses. Are you just using me till I run dry?

The two stared into each other's eyes.

You've been baptized, haven't you? When?

When I was thirteen. In Tokyo.

When you were thirteen. At the Tokyo Holy Resurrection Cathedral?

Right.

So you weren't baptized as an infant. The woman brushed the hair back from the youth's eyes.

It wasn't an infant baptism. My parents are Japanese, so they gave me the freedom to choose my own faith.

You were baptized in a Japanese church, in the Japanese style. You bowed down, and the priest wetted your forehead. There was no full-body submersion. You were quiet, like a sheep at the shearer.

That's right.

And then your parents turned around, turned their backs on the icons, and spat on Satan. Didn't they?

That's right.

Do you remember anything else from when you were thirteen?

Not much. It's all a blur. I remember all the house parties, practically every night. My mother would invite everyone from the congregation and treat them all to an oversized pirog.

Were those parties painful for you?

The laughter. The sound of people sipping vodka, chewing meat. My parents, their friends, my grandparents, all encouraging me to eat more. They always said I was too thin, too pale, too unhealthy.

But you didn't want to eat.

No. All they ever talked about was the church. Can we use olive oil when fasting? Are sticharions for the Pentecost made in Greece or Russia? Should we place candlesticks near the incorruptible body?

But you didn't say anything. You turned pale, and felt nauseated by all the food placed in front of you.

Eventually, the conversation turned to a madwoman someone saw at Ochanomizu Station on the way over.

I know her. She was there when I still went to church. She was mentally ill, and was struggling with some sort of family trouble, but she was still sound of mind. Her speech was coherent, and she could still laugh. I heard that she was hospitalized, but then one day she came to Ochanomizu Station dressed in rags. She must have escaped.

Just as I was kissing the cross, the woman started screaming over at the station, and an ambulance came to pick her up. Some of the congregation members heard the sirens. I was in the sanctuary, so I didn't. But that day, I learned about her mental illness for myself. I wanted to see her. But then that was the end of the conversation, and everyone started talking about other things.

But you weren't interested in any of those.

I was thinking about why crazy people scream, and how they're driven to insanity. I wanted to know.

You say you wanted to know. You already knew, and yet still you say you wanted to.

As soon as I learned about her mental illness, she stopped coming to Ochanomizu. Because of the iconostasis, I couldn't hear the sound of the ambulance carrying her away. If I had seen her, I would have shared in her madness, I would have let myself go crazy too. It's a strange story.

So, miraculously, you missed your chance to sympathize with her.

I don't know if I'm fortunate or not, but ever since I was a child, I've never been put in an environment where I might be tempted by insanity.

In other words, you lived in an environment where you wouldn't end up like that woman.

In the time of the Old Testament, it was believed that madmen were possessed by evil spirits. And that the reason for their madness was that they, or a family member, had sinned. When Christ came to us in the body of man, he disavowed that belief. But my family still lives in the Old Testament.

It's a sin to go mad in your family.

Yes, it is. No one feels sorry for you. All they do is despise you. I had a fight with my brother once. I hit him. That was enough to make me fear my own actions.

A small emotional outburst isn't worthy of madness. But you still feared it, didn't you? Because even that was unforgivable.

My head went fuzzy, and I couldn't hear anything. I had a vision that the floor had risen up to my knees, and then I passed out.

You're like a toy. A pale, organic toy that turns off when it overheats.

But there *are* people who scream out loud when they can't express malice in words. Like that woman.

And some people die.

You're thinking about someone in particular, aren't you?

The woman didn't respond.

I wish that I was dead too, sometimes.

You couldn't.

That's right. I realize that all too well. . . Were you comparing me to someone just now?

The woman didn't respond.

You're like a fortune teller. Everything you say about me is spot on.

We're both sound of mind, that's all.

You're just like me. Someone, someone immensely powerful, robbed you of your chance to scream, to go insane.

Yes. But the details aren't important. Its significance, when it happened, or who exploited me. I've already forgotten most of it.

It's true that neither of us is endowed with the power of memory.

Memory. . . Yes. We try so hard to remember. We build memorial parks and museums to remind ourselves of malice. But now they've become places for children to play.

Did you know? The arms of the Peace Statue make a right angle. Not even children absorbed in their games will be able to forget the straight lines made by those arms.

A right angle? Ninety degrees? I wonder what exactly in Nagasaki was ninety degrees that day? Maybe the darkness of deep disorder that gripped people's hearts? I saw some sewing needles that had been melted together. Not at all at ninety degrees. Each and every painful thorn bunched together into an indescribable shape. Not even a shape like that would be able to describe this city. But a right angle. . . Yes. No one ever forgets a right angle. Not even children preoccupied with their games. What a wonderful geometric pattern the mushroom cloud made. But I don't remember what shape that mass of sewing needles was anymore. No one can remember. You can cry, but you can't remember. Because that shape is too irregular. Oh! How irregular our past! But it's because it's so irregular that we're able to forget. That's why we're sane.

The woman touched the youth's face as though blind, examining its irregularities. Its steep and gentle slopes.

Nagasaki is filled with slopes, isn't it? They go up and down. Irregular, steep, gentle slopes. I like your shape. We can't remember the momentary shape of the drink we shared with the one who violated our flesh, the domed architecture under which we prostrated ourselves, the wave that the screaming woman made—but we know that our shapes overlap perfectly. You and I would be lost as two figures among a thousand sane people. No one will distinguish you or me. I won't distinguish between you and me either.

Nor will I be able to distinguish myself from you.

That's right. The woman stared into the youth. So this is what it means to meet someone so alike. Up till now, I was certainly sane. I had never thought about dying. I was too afraid. But I'm thinking about dying now. When I look at you, at you, so similar to me, I feel like my life is about to be snatched away. I feel like I want to become one with you. Completely. No, I want to be absorbed by you. That's the best way to put it, yes. I feel like I don't even need myself anymore. It's. . .desire. It's definitely desire. I'm lusting to touch your body. I feel like I'm in love with you. But it's so clear to me. Nothing is born from two people so alike falling in love with one another. By becoming one with you, I'm trying to kill myself. Me loving you means two similar people loving each other, and that gives birth only to death.

But in fact, if we made love together in a room, nothing would happen.

Yes. But I'm. . .a coward. I can't die making love with you. For us, that room where we make love is the lower bound of order.

And we have to part ways before we exceed that lower bound of order.

That's right.

You are disorder, just like me. You'll devour my body, and in the end, you'll abandon me.

That's true.

The woman took a sip of her Kir. Then, at a loss, she stared into the distance.

Disorder just like me. Is that really your body? Isn't it this land itself, this state of being, those things that make no sense put together, that mass of melted glass bottles, the corpses of children burned beyond recognition, innumerable skulls piled up like rubbish? Is it a human body that I'm devouring? Really? Isn't it this state of being, this land. . .Nagasaki? It's Nagasaki that I'm devouring. And you, no one, you . . . are Nagasaki.

Nagasaki, that's my name.

Maybe I'll dismantle you. Maybe then I'll find meaning. Each and every piece of your past rolling around like the head of a statue of a saint destroyed in the blast. I'll study them all, analyze them. As though they were all piled up intentionally. Because maybe they were. Maybe someone piled them together under some special law. But I can't understand their meaning. I call that state Nagasaki. And that state is you.

The woman and the youth held each other, naked, pressing their lips against each other's bodies.

When do you leave Nagasaki? the youth asked.

I haven't decided. In the not-too-distant future.

Will you marry me?

The woman laughed. We can't, she said. I'm not baptized. You'll want to hold the ceremony in your church, no?

My parents got married there. You don't like it?

I didn't say that. The woman gently pinched the youth's cheek. But I already told you. I'm leaving Nagasaki soon. That will be the end of our relationship.

Have you ever seen a man who gorges himself on prostitutes? Doesn't that kind of person strike you as ridiculous, vacuous even?

The woman separated her body from his. She averted her gaze, turning her attention to the past. The image of a man appeared in her mind's eye. A man who replaced one lover with another, who engaged in an endless stream of affairs. He always cried when it was over. As though *he* had been defiled. A vagina slept in the depths of that person's heart. A hole—dark, deep, never moist. Who had violated him? When?

You despise yourself as a whore. And you pity yourself. For being raped by a filthy woman.

The woman grabbed the youth's hair, and stared into his eyes.

That's right.

The youth turned his face away. Like a small child in a self-pitying sulk.

You were a whore. Yes, a whore.

The woman loosened her fingers around the youth's hair. The youth's weight sank into the bed.

You humiliate yourself that way, don't you? You despise yourself, unconsciously. That's what makes me act obscene. It makes me want you. You make me want to take that poor, reviled body of yours, and place my own body on top of it.

The woman put the youth's genitals in her mouth. She could feel their movements through her teeth. Blood gathered inside them. The youth moved his legs, grabbed the woman's hair, and interrupted what she was doing. As though insulted. His eyes squeezed firmly shut.

The youth's genitals were in her mouth. The woman's breathing grew irregular. Her consciousness dimmed. The youth's panting voice overlapped with that of someone from her past. *His* panting voice. He often brought his lovers to his room. His room was next to hers. He used to say that no matter how many women whom he took to bed, it would never be enough. He was a stupid man. Ignorant of his own hunger. He believed that it was others who satisfied him. When he couldn't find enough satisfaction, he would reach for one person after another. And so he defiled his own body. He doubted his own eyes. He saw his partners' bodies as clean. As though they possessed a strong mucous membrane capable of wiping away the filth. Did his partners consider that act sacred? Did he, who loved only himself, think that he could receive love from another? In any event, he couldn't defile his partner's bodies. They remained clean, while his misery of mind and body endured. His alone.

The youth threw himself atop the woman. The youth, who called himself a whore, now wanted to ruin himself even more. He wanted to reduce himself, to demean his heart and body in the face of this unattainable love. That was all that he could think to do.

The act of coupling, the insertion of the genitals, was painful for both of them. The youth had probably forgotten that he had ever loved the woman. He was empty, hollow, left with no choice but to attack her for having insulted him. With the one meager weapon that he possessed. He was a child blaming others for his innate loneliness. He didn't even realize how much he would regret it later. His breath was ragged. He looked as though he were about to die of pleasure, of pain. The woman saw Nagasaki in his body. Deep chaos and disorder.

Eventually, the youth was spent, and collapsed into her. The woman wrapped her arms around his back. Her hands slid over his sweat.

I was just thinking about something terribly sacrilegious, the woman whispered to him.

It wouldn't be long before the youth realized the repulsive nature of what he had just done, and that realization would drive him mad.

I was thinking. About this land.

The youth didn't respond. His breath was heavy with effort.

I was thinking about this land, while we had intercourse.

The woman held the youth's head to her.

This is sacrilege.

Once their intercourse was complete, the youth went to take a shower. The numbing sound of the shower washed painfully over the woman's body. The youth always washed his body after having sex. Carefully. Attentively. Because of his atopy. When he stepped out of the shower, he applied ointment. Then he lay naked on the bed for a while, until his body dried. The youth harbored various feelings of inferiority, but he was indifferent only to his nakedness. He lay there naked, like Adam in the Garden of Eden.

There are numerous icons of Mary the Theotokos in the Tokyo Holy Resurrection Cathedral. One of them, located by the Saint Nicholas Chapel, is said to shed tears. When looking at her carefully, one can find something like scratch marks under her eyes. The glass-paned icon is impervious to scratches, so it is said that the Theotokos sheds tears. The faithful, who trust that their belief can move mountains, don't find anything shocking in the tears of the Theotokos. Nonetheless, a great many of them offer her candles.

There was a woman who prayed fervently to the Weeping Theotokos. But was *praying* the right word? She always appeared there in the middle of the evening service, lit candles, and stared at the Theotokos for a short while. By the end of the service, she would have disappeared. That's the Matushka, one of the parishioners told me. The Matushka. A noun tinged with anonymity. A Russian word meaning *woman* or *mother*, similar to the French *madame*. In the Church, the wives of all the priests were known by that title. It wasn't meant to be a proper noun.

The Matushka always offered candles to the Weeping Theotokos. What kind of sorrow did she harbor? To me, this woman, whose proper noun I didn't know, was nothing less than sorrow itself. I had no choice but to name this nameless woman the Weeping Theotokos.

Most of my memories are of my brother's suffering. My own proper nouns have been stripped away. His name replaced them. He took a great many things from me. My name was just one of them. My everyday concerns, my own private matters. My brother's madness was everything, and occupied most of my consciousness. I was a pitiful bird that had forgotten how to sing. My cry had become his. When he died, when I was finally ready to live my own life, I realized that I didn't know how to sob in my own voice, how to speak in my own words.

The bird called man sings in his own voice, speaks in his own words. I thought that I could offer my voice, which my brother had taken from me, to another man. I didn't think to sing in my own voice, to speak in my own words. I didn't care what kind of man he was. I searched for a creature that could turn the disorder that my brother had left inside me into order, even if only a false pretense. A creature that could turn *something* into words. Perhaps I was a fool, but I told every man whom I met about my brother, about my chaotic suffering over him. Some tried to brush off my past as vulgar, to jump straight to intercourse. Others were kind enough to point out that it was a particularly somber past, to recognize that I was still suffering from it. But none claimed to be unable to express it, or argued that it made no sense. Just as I had expected, these brilliant artists had placed a melody in the heart of this mediocre woman.

Mediocrity is a pronoun given to disorder when all else fails. It is like calling a non-existent color white, or labelling an illness an allergic reaction when you don't know its name. If a man were to call a woman's past mediocre, a woman whose alcoholic brother ended his own life, what choice do I have but to accept that label? Inside me, the meaning of my brother's actions is disjointed. Why did he cry that time? What meaning lay behind his misdeeds? His unfathomable sensual desire? His cause of death? With that, my general notion of mad behavior is destroyed. My own depression began with just such a denial of meaning. When I remember my brother, the causes underlying the chain of my own emotions, my loneliness, my fear, my anxiety, become uncertain. I'm desperate to find a reason for these feelings. If I don't, I'm as good as dead. I manage to survive day-to-day by giving a false sense of order to the disorder, by lulling myself into a momentary sense of security. By relying on a man whom I may or may not even like.

The woman and the youth woke up the following morning in each other's arms. The youth's body was damp with sweat. He took a shower to meticulously wash himself clean. When he finished, he stepped out naked, wiping his body with a towel.

He lay face-down on the bed, and allowed his body to dry exposed to the air. The woman rubbed an ointment of clobetasol propionate over his back.

You've decided not to hide your skin from me anymore, haven't you? That's why you're letting me apply your medicine to it, no? You've entrusted your skin into my hands, the woman said. Thanks to my skin condition, I can sense, intuitively, whether someone means to hurt me, the youth responded. You don't. At least not my skin.

I can sense that too, you know? Even without your condition. I can tell the difference between someone who wants to do me harm and someone who doesn't.

We're like small animals, ready to flee on a moment's notice, the youth said. That's right. The woman's hands kept moving. That's the privilege of the weak.

Have you ever been bullied over it? the woman asked.

Plenty of times. Especially in the summer. Like when we had swimming lessons at school. I don't like going into the water at swimming pools. It seeps into my skin. And people notice it when I go swimming. They whisper to each other, and point at me. But they don't do anything, not yet. Because the teacher is watching. They wait until we go back to the changing room, after class. The teacher isn't around then. Everyone keeps their distance from me, talking about my atopy, saying that I'm contagious. One of them steals my swimsuit, and keeps passing it around as if it's soiled. I want to get changed as quickly as I can, but someone has thrown my clothes into the trash. So I'm naked, and they all laugh at me.

The girls too? the woman asked.

The girls too. Gender doesn't matter in that kind of situation. When a girl finds a man weaker than she is, she forgets that she would have been the weaker of the two in terms of gender. That's especially the case with children. They don't realize yet that women are at a disadvantage.

That's right. The woman's hand came to a stop on the youth's back. You come across women like that every now and then. The kind who act like they were brought up on pure malice. That kind who grew up never realizing that women are weak.

There is no such thing as a woman who isn't attracted to

other women. Those who tell themselves that they aren't have simply failed to realize it. But they are the lucky ones. If a woman realizes that she is attracted to other women, she won't be able to compromise with a man with whom she can be only moderately comfortable.

The woman with whom I fell in love left a horrible first impression. But that happens all the time. If it were a man, I would definitely choose someone who left a good first impression. But with a woman, it isn't so easy. I was curious about this woman who left the worst possible impression on me. She would gather people around her and go out for drinks, speak ill of others behind their backs, and gossip about everyone else's secrets. I was afraid of her malice. When she drank, she would shed tears, and complain that she was all alone. Alone. If she were a man, I would never have gotten involved with her. But I sympathized with her, and so every now and then, I would drive her home.

One day, I dropped her off at home just like usual. She was so drunk that I had to carry her up to her bed. When I sat her down, she began to kiss me, as though trying to bite my lips off. No part of me thought that this was insane. Because she was always committing transgressions. As she kissed me, she squeezed my breasts so hard that they hurt. I consented to this act. As though all her malice existed solely to squeeze my breasts. That was the only time that I ever had intercourse with a woman.

That was the only time that I ever sympathized with another person's malice. The intense pleasure that I received then has since transformed into regret and anguish. I realize now that I live in a world inhabited by pleasant men and compromise.

Why don't you get dressed? the woman asked. I've finished applying your ointment, and you're already dry. The youth turned over languidly. I want to stay this way a while longer, he said. I thought you said people used to bully you, and steal your clothes? And yet you're still happy to lie naked in front of others.

I want to stay this way a while longer, the youth said. I mean, *you* won't make fun of my skin, will you?

I'm not without malice, you know? If you stay that way too long, I might say something terrible. Like those girls used to.

I've already forgotten them. The youth smiled.

They ate breakfast in the hotel restaurant on the first floor. The same place as yesterday. A breakfast buffet.

The youth filled his tray with yogurt, fruit, and a glass of apple juice. You're only eating sweets? the woman asked. You're only eating Japanese food, the youth commented.

The youth reached across his tray to pick up his glass of apple juice. The woman stole a glimpse of his arms inside his shirt sleeves. His damaged skin.

I was relieved when you got dressed, the woman said. Why? Because if you stayed naked any longer, I would probably have said something cruel about your skin.

I'm sure you would have. The youth kept his gaze lowered as he spooned up a helping of yogurt. But you said you had forgotten? the woman asked. Yes. Why?

Because it was too unreasonable. It exceeded my capacity to remember. Like an irregular sequence of numbers. Like the number pi, or the way the Western calendar cuts through history. There's no way to remember any of that unless you can hammer it home with a mnemonic or something. Once you've been gone for a few days, I'll probably forget that you ever even held me.

Are you angry? No. Even though it's so unreasonable? Unreasonableness doesn't warrant getting angry.

The woman stirred her iced coffee with her straw, staring into the confusion. So it's not worth getting angry over.

Unreasonableness. The woman chewed over that word. She wondered whether there really was such a thing. She didn't know.

What's wrong? The youth's voice brought her back to herself. Nothing. The woman laughed. I was just thinking about when I was younger. I was always fighting with my family over one unreasonable thing or another.

When someone says something unreasonable to me, I can't bring myself to get into a fight over it, the youth said. I'm not very smart, so I guess I can't point out where the other person is wrong.

The youth had penetrated her with his genitals. The woman had thought that he must have been crazy with regret. Their intercourse had produced nothing. Two cells with similar properties had become one. The boundaries between them had disappeared. Two bodies reduced to one. Not life, but death. Not even love. Merely a process of amalgamation. She had assumed that the youth would be unable to endure such an unreasonable process. But could he? Heaven had bestowed on him stupidity and grit. He couldn't remember unreasonableness, he said. Nor would he remember their act of intercourse, symbolizing sheer meaninglessness.

No matter how many times I read it, I can never remember the Book of Job. A righteous man named Job is put through countless trials, and complains to God. And so God appears before Job, rebuking him. It is at that moment that Job regains his faith. What I can't remember are the passages describing Job's trials, nor God's excuse for why he must endure them.

What are your plans for today? the youth asked. I'm not going anywhere. I didn't come here to go sightseeing. Maybe I'll wander around the hotel, or stay in my room, the woman responded. What you're saying is that you aren't leaving Nagasaki today? the youth asked. That's right.

Good. In that case, why don't you join me this afternoon? I'm going to see the Chinatown this morning, but I'll be back after that. I don't mind, the woman answered. The youth flashed her a relieved smile.

What exactly was he thinking? the woman wondered. Why did he still want to meet her? They had engaged in meaningless intercourse, but he wasn't downhearted or hurt. That alone should have been fortunate enough for him. He should flee from her before his luck ran out. That would have been how any normal person would have reacted. But the youth wanted to see her again, he said. They might find themselves engaging in intercourse once more. She wondered whether he understood that.

All of a sudden, the youth poured his apple juice into her iced coffee.

What was that for? The woman covered the cup with her hand. You were zoning out, so I thought I'd make you laugh. The youth smiled. You looked kind of sad. Did you remember something unpleasant?

Perhaps she *was* sad. This foolish, defenseless youth was certainly sad. Various folktales, all revolving around one fool or another, flooded the woman's head. This was the first time that she had ever felt pity for a man. The men whom she had known were narcissistic angels who didn't require pity, despicable men who deserved not pity but hatred, and intelligent, strong-minded husbands who always kept pity at arm's length.

I'll buy you a souvenir, the youth said.

The woman took a stroll around the hotel. She found a small nursery school. There were no atomic bombs in the pasts of these children. Probably not even in the lives of the nursery teachers. In this nursery school, once the sight of the atomic bombing, a child squealed with delight on a swing. The nursery teacher counted the number of swings as she pushed the child back and forth. One. Two. Three. Four.

Spring is hot in Nagasaki. The woman was thirsty. She felt like eating a bowl of shaved ice. Perhaps there was a café nearby? She remembered the museum. Right, the tearoom there sold shaved ice. Not that she planned to go back, however.

The tearoom at the museum was on the first basement floor. Next to the restrooms. She had stared at it from a distance on her way to the toilet. The display window had been decorated not only with coffees and shaved ice, but castella cakes too. There were two groups each of three or four ladies inside. They hadn't looked like tourists. It had seemed strange to the woman that locals would visit a place like this on a weekday. After a while, she had realized that these ladies were using the museum in lieu of a café. She had felt ill-at-ease at the idea of visiting a place like this for such a purpose. It was an incredibly ordinary sight. In the tearoom, the ladies had laughed, had eaten shaved ice, and had chatted brightly with each other. The permanent exhibition was on the second basement floor, slumbering beneath the tearoom. The place with the replica of the Fat Man bomb and the pictures of women with their hair falling out.

One. Two. Three. Four. The nursery teacher was now pushing another child on the swing. The children were taking turns after a certain number of pushes. The body of Nagasaki carefully conceals all trace of its scars. Like a beautiful young woman who has been badly beaten. Foundation applied neatly over her bruises. Her lips painted with rouge. She successfully makes herself look more beautiful even than a healthy girl. I can't remember that unreasonableness. Those had been the youth's words. The woman wondered whether he had been telling the truth. But it went beyond merely forgetting. If one has truly forgotten, if one's memory is a blank canvas, from where comes that stubborn urge to paint over all traces of violence? From where arises that unconscious power of discernment that allows one not only to erase violence, but also to hide it from others?

This is how my memory works. I remember what happened in the past. As accurately as possible.

I don't have many good memories. Most of them are sad or painful. I'm sure that the same could be said for most people. I'm not satisfied just with superficial events. I try to faithfully recreate my perceptions as much as possible. I try my hand at fleshing out the impressions that remain. The time that my mother slapped me. Her firm, wrinkled hand. My nose bled, that time. The ugly, miserable look on her face. How did it come to that? It doesn't matter. My mother would always hit me until my nose bled, all for no sensible reason. After a while, I would point out to her that she had hit me over nothing. She would say that I was exaggerating. She would say that she never hit me until my nose bled. I would say nothing. Because I knew that she honestly couldn't remember. I couldn't blame her. Because all that she remembered was spoiling me. But I found the ambivalence of my mother's memory terrifying. I began to drink. When I got drunk, everything seemed so much better, and I felt as though I could throw myself from some high place. I wanted to have intercourse with whomever I could find.

Eventually, I realized it. Whose perceptions were these? They belonged to my brother. Words that recall memories. Every time that I try to recreate these perceptions through words, the grounded subject that is me floats away, and the subject of my brother sets its feet firmly on the ground. From word to word. As I translate the facts, as I render them with yet greater accuracy and fidelity, the subject of the action changes from me to my brother. My memories become distorted by the violence of words.

That is why I cover my memories with makeup. Beautifully. I paint over them, as though nothing ever happened. I tolerate not how my mother beat me, but the violence of the words, which have distorted even their subject by contradicting all memory. And so I decided to forgive. Whenever I recall the past, I can't remember whether it was me or my brother who suffered. Sometimes, I tell it without knowing the answer. It is as though it isn't even my story. As though it is all made up. That is why confessing my past to people brings no mutual understanding. It is a made-up past. Yet what I really want them to know are the bruises hidden behind my makeup. This history of abuse.

The woman gave up on the idea of shaved ice and bought a sandwich and a popsicle to eat in her room. She looked over her room again. A room with only her in it. A room without the youth. Immaculate. Elegant. But there was something cool and silent about it. She remembered reading how the rooms in this hotel were supposed to recreate the semblance of a monastery. Ah, she thought. This would be a good place to pray.

Remembering that she had promised to meet the youth that afternoon, she took a look at her face in the bathroom. She had been sweating, considerably. Her makeup was at risk of coming off.

Staring at her own face in the mirror, the woman's emotions stood still. She had no impression of the self in the reflection. When she was younger, she used to examine herself in the mirror, and criticize this feature or that. How she liked the strength of her eyes, but not her raised cheekbones. That sort of thing. Her mother praised her face when they were at home. It wasn't a bad face, she said. But she never praised her in front of others. Oh, she isn't at all a beauty. She takes too much after me, I'm afraid. If only she could have inherited her father's looks. And so her mother's distorted humility wounded the young woman, until she gradually gave up on the idea of becoming beautiful.

Ever since then, mirrors lost their power to instill in the woman any sense of superiority or inferiority. For her, they were merely reflections of something that looked just like her. A figure on the other side of a sheet of glass, who would one day replace her. The woman had heard countless stories like that. But she never realized that they were ghost stories. She stared into the mirror. Mesmerized. Wondering when the reflection on the other side would take her place.

I had intercourse with my brother, in my mind. Over and over again. I was lost with desire for him. But it wasn't me with whom he was having sex. It was other women. My brother, though consumed with self-love, engaged in intercourse with other women. Whenever he saw a woman, he would think for a brief moment that he was in love with her. Eventually, he would come to his senses, remember that he loved only himself, and abandon her. That was how it always played out. The women's stubborn attachments came in all different forms. But eventually, they would realize that my brother was a man who loved only himself, and then they would leave.

I knew it. That my brother was avoiding me.

I was always observing his lovers, carefully. My brother's sexual partners were women who, like him, were possessed by self-love. Women who loved only themselves, who never truly drew close to my brother. There was always a wall that separated them from him. One couldn't say that they had chemistry, not even as an act of hollow flattery. But the source of my brother's rationality lay in that wall. For a while, he would behave like a decent young man. He would drink less and less. Eventually, the moment of intercourse would arrive. In the process of breaking down that wall of reason, my brother would destroy himself. He would insert his member into the woman's vagina. He wouldn't be able to stand the foreign object tightening around him. A person who can't love others. But he could only sleep with such women. That contradiction would be thrust before him, and the wall of his reason would collapse. My brother would hate himself. And he would bury those abominable memories together with those self-loving women.

If I had intercourse with my brother, if I, his shadow, had intercourse with him, I was sure that our bodies would be a perfect fit. But my brother avoided me. He was afraid that if we had sex, he would become a false reflection of me.

The woman glanced around the bathroom. The bar of soap had shrunk considerably. She had never used so much in a hotel before. The youth always showered after intercourse. His atopy was eating away at his pale half-Russian skin. His disease wasn't the only thing eating away at that skin. It was undoubtedly stained by the hands of countless women. The woman was no different. She had been stained by the hands of countless men. But the woman and the youth hadn't dyed each other's skin. Their skin met. The youth's name, Nagasaki, was the same as having no name at all. As was the woman's. She was just a housewife. And yet in this land she didn't even possess the title of housewife. They were both nothing. They didn't love themselves. The woman didn't seek love from the youth. And the youth claimed that he would be unable to recall their unreasonable congress.

The woman and the youth were still sane. Though their bodies had intertwined, they were both still sane. Because neither of them loved themselves.

The woman's married life is filled with events like this. One day, she went to a toy store and bought the biggest Christmas tree that she could find. It was needlessly large for her three-year-old child. She bought it for herself. There was a shining star at its top, ornaments in the shape of empty gift boxes, and balls of all the primary colors that made her head feel dizzy. The woman was spellbound by the false, dazzling glow of those ornaments. Her husband was more than a little surprised when he laid eyes on that Christmas tree. It's so big. You bought it for the child? he asked.

That's right, the woman answered. Christmas is a big event for children. Besides, it would cost more to buy another one when he gets bigger, don't you think?

I see. You're a good mother. Did you buy it with your allowance? The woman nodded. I'll pay for it. My bonus came in today. Her husband laughed.

And so the woman acquired the tree. Simply. With her husband's money. She marveled that there were men like this in the world. A more discerning man might have called it wasteful, a needlessly huge Christmas tree. You just wanted it for yourself, he might have said. You're out of your mind. But her husband didn't say anything like that.

The woman busied herself preparing for Christmas. Ornaments depicting the Nativity. Joseph and Mary, standing on either side of a manger. Why isn't there anything in the box? the child asked her. They're looking forward to Christmas, the woman answered. She bought an advent calendar for the child. He opened the paper windows one by one, starting on the first of December. Inside, he found pictures of goats and sheep. The window for the twenty-fourth was especially large. Can I open it? the child asked, pointing at it. No, she said, gripping his impatient finger. Not until the twenty-fourth. I wonder what's inside, the child murmured. The woman smiled.

And so Christmas arrived. A doll of the baby Jesus appeared in the manger. Cherubim and seraphim, the Three Wise Men of the East, and Christ himself were all found behind the twenty-fourth door on the advent calendar. The woman bought a turkey from the delicatessen. She decorated a bûche de Noël with whipped cream. She prepared some ginger fried chicken and sushi rolls, and placed them on the table.

At dinnertime, her husband returned home with presents and a bottle of champagne. The child ran up to him in anticipation of his gift. Her husband handed it to him.

When her husband came to the table, the woman poured the champagne into a pair of flutes. Her husband handed her a present. The woman, not having expected to receive anything, startled. Inside the box was a diamond necklace. You don't have any jewelry for when we go out on dates, do you? You can wear this next time.

Dates. The woman and her husband went out on those dates for no reason at all. Her husband would find a nice, fancy restaurant, and the woman would wear her best clothes for the occasion. Those clothes were her husband's selection. They couldn't have been cheap, but as he had paid for them, she had no way of knowing for sure. She would no doubt wear this diamond necklace too on their next such date.

Her husband cast his gaze over the table. Talk about a feast, he said. As though only then remembering, the woman wiped away her sweat and took off her apron. She let out a heavy sigh as she watched her husband swallow a sushi roll. She urged him to try the chicken. She had fried the pieces one by one. One. Two. Three. Four. All in stoic silence.

After lunch, the woman fell into a deep sleep. A chime rang. She woke up. There was a knock at the door. She opened it. The youth was standing there, laughing. She remembered the promise that she had made to meet him that afternoon. The youth held a paper bag up to her face.

The woman turned her back to him, and walked deeper

into the room. She didn't say anything. No *Come inside*, no *Please*. Excuse me, the youth said as he stepped through the doorway.

The woman sat down on the bed, in silence. The youth sat on the sofa across from her. He endured the silence. Smiling. Flashing her his ivory-white teeth. I brought you a souvenir, he whispered eventually. He handed the woman the paper bag. Inside was a loquat jelly and a bottle of shōchū. Really? she asked. You didn't have to go to Chinatown to get these. Don't you know they sell them in the airport? It couldn't be helped, the youth responded. If you had come with me, we could have eaten champon noodles and dim sum, and I wouldn't have had to buy a souvenir.

That's true. The woman rose to her feet. In that case, let's share the jelly. I'll make some tea. No, the youth said, urging her to sit back down. I'll do it.

The youth suddenly turned his eyes to the desk. You went to Urakami Cathedral, didn't you? he asked, picking up a pamphlet.

Ah, the woman murmured. The day I went to the museum. I went for a bit of a stroll beforehand. It was just a normal church. Except for the atomic bombing.

You must have seen the statue of the broken saint, right?

Yes. On the surface, it looks like a ruined church. But the inside was beautiful. You could hold a good mass in there. As if nothing had ever happened. There were piles of broken relics and the heads of statues of saints in the Pietà Congregation Hall. Chalices, soft and warped like pieces of candy. I was surprised to see the church left those sacred artifacts like that. They left the memories of the bombing alone, without trying to restore them.

Catholics remember the Passion more strongly than they do the Resurrection.

That's right. There was a statue of Christ with his arms and legs broken off on display. People probably cry so hard when they see it. They probably all forget that he was resurrected three days later. The memory of the church that we know is the icon of the Resurrection, the one painted on the iconostasis. The Victory of Christ. But the mural in the church here is of Christ being tried by Pontius Pilate, of him being nailed to the cross.

It's called the Via Crucis, the Way of the Cross.

It's a symbol. But an incredibly vague one. Ambiguous. It made me think not only of the tragedy of the atomic bomb, but also the Passion, the Resurrection, things like that. I saw a statue of Mary that made it through the bombing. It was enshrined in the chapel. But it had no eyes. She lost her eyes to the bombing. She was expressionless. As if wearing a mask. It was the exact opposite of the statue of Our Lady of Peace with her hands together in prayer. Just a blank mask. That Mary must be the sky above. The Mary of Nagasaki isn't thinking anything. She doesn't even think about peace. She just stands there, in a daze. Who could have predicted such a thing?

What you're saying is you saw a mask that symbolizes nothing.

It doesn't symbolize anything, no. . . A broken statue of Mary would surely win people's sympathy. But it just looks like an empty mask, like a road sign, like an intellectual objet d'art, like the alphabet of an unknown country. It isn't meaningless. No, it's filled with too many meanings. Those meanings keep rolling over each other in turns, never settling. I feel like this has been on my mind for so long, ever since I decorated the Christmas tree in my small apartment. Because it isn't about the statue of Mary. It's about everything, and that includes me. If you decide on just one meaning, you deny everything else. One meaning is associated with another, and then denied. And so on, forever. In the end, I don't know what lies behind anything anymore. The more I keep thinking about it, the more confused it makes me, the more frustrated, and then I see that mushroom cloud. My intuition kicks in the moment I think of it as beautiful. I came to this land because I doubted that feeling, because I wanted, desperately, to instill in my mind a more tragic image of Nagasaki. I hadn't accepted that there could be so many meanings, all whirling around so dizzyingly. It was like I was trying to create an image of myself, by living in a small apartment complex, by dressing myself in an apron. And you tried to stabilize my impressions. Pitiful Nagasaki. Me, living in an apartment complex.

The woman clung to the youth's neck. The youth stroked her neck.

The apartment block, that apron, they connect me to myself, but they aren't everything. The red of the wine that dyes the whiteness of the apron, the blood shed during intercourse. But some things don't have any color at all. Bones like stainless steel, silk wrapped around my body. This isn't color. It's texture. The skin of a potato. It's a position. My position. The biggest part of this chain is something unimportant, something that I want to get rid of, as soon as possible. Me. Myself. These things have left me. Rootless weeds. They'll drift further and further away from me. But I'll watch them. Not just me. Every one of those rootless weeds. You, a chanson singer, a crowd, a pipe, a dance, a broken heart, violence, experience. Their meanings replaced by other meanings, always changing.

The woman rested her hand against the youth's cheek, staring at him. I'm scared, she murmured.

I'm nobody. An unimportant, disgusting woman. I've known it for so long. Though only vaguely. It's chance that decides what kind of woman I'll be today. It isn't up to me. I was like a corpse. But then I realized that everything was like a corpse. The meaning behind everything is decided by a throw of the dice. Dice thrown haphazardly. Everyone accepts the outcome, whatever happens, without resistance. It's just. . .

Right! What else can you call it but a corpse? A pall has fallen over the world. I'm staring into the Apocalypse. And the world is bleached white. Made white so that it can be dyed by chance. But you already knew that, didn't you? You're just like me, so you must have realized it, haven't you?

The youth didn't respond. He brushed her hair over her ears. You're wearing makeup today, aren't you? You look beautiful.

The woman nodded, trembling. Thinking that she had angered him.

Your eyeshadow is particularly vivid. What color is it? It looks like a mix between blue and navy.

It's called Cool Sky, the woman murmured faintly.

But it would look so sad for someone with skin as pale as yours to wear this color, this Cool Sky. Are your tears this color, I wonder?

The youth kissed her eyelids.

Hey. You should be scared too, right?

The woman began to unbutton his shirt. The youth moved to unbutton the rest. One by one, as though embarrassed.

Your skin knows the same fears that I do. It suits me.

The woman rested her cheek against the youth's bare chest.

You smell nice today. Because you're wearing makeup, I wonder?

I put on some perfume. I do things like this sometimes, on a whim. You've realized it, haven't you? That the world ended long ago?

The only thing I smell like is the frankincense in the cathedral. I should have worn perfume too.

You should have.

You don't like the smell of frankincense?

That's not the point.

The woman breathed in the scent of the youth's skin. She knew. The scent of frankincense was only on his clothes. Not on his naked flesh. The scent of frankincense would undoubtedly seep into the sticharion of anyone who played the role of altar server, as the youth did. But the woman breathed it in. As though trying to convince him that the scent of frankincense had permeated his body. Thanks to that gesture, the youth believed that the scent had indeed permeated his body. He tried to pull away from her. The woman clung to him, and laid him down on the bed. She nuzzled her face into his chest.

There's nothing I can say.

The woman glanced up at the sound of the youth's voice.

Not about the horrors you experienced.

The woman narrowed her eyes. Her eyelids were covered with eyeshadow. Cool Sky. The color of tears.

I won't say anything. But you'll probably end up thinking it. That I'm no different than all those men who passed you by.

The woman stared at the youth.

But you've been humiliated so much. By men. I know.

Then answer me, please. Say something, about what I just told you.

The youth shook his head.

My past is rootless. My impressions change from one to the next. No sooner do they summon joy than they turn to pain. No sooner do they seem comfortably pale than they become blindingly vivid. I don't know what kind of person my brother was anymore. Mad or sane, kind or cruel, lustful or austere. I don't know my brother, and I don't know myself. My brother has always been the person on the other side of the mirror. My perception of myself has always been relative to how I see him. I look at my brother first, and then by comparing myself against him, I know myself. That was how my mother taught me to perceive myself. You're better at studying than your brother, she used to say to me. You're better behaved than your brother. When she said that, I thought to myself: I see. I see. I earned more A grades on my report card than he did. My homeroom teacher never called my mother about me breaking the rules at school like he did. That was why I never had any dreams of my own about what I might like to do for a career when I grew up. All that I knew was that I could study a little bit better than he could. I didn't even know if I was attractive. I was just a student who didn't break any of the rules.

My mother loved my brother more than she did me. She loved only him. I don't know why. I understood, at some vague level, that he was attractive. So I gave up. I could never match his charm. I would let him have my mother's love. I swore to myself that I would love him as much as my mother did. My mother created my brother first. She gave him his existence. A perfect existence. She never doubted how much she needed him. No matter how much he misbehaved, he was her child, her adorable child, and so she kept him by her side. And so thinking, she gave him life. Next, she made me. She made me in the image of my brother, but she didn't need me with the same compulsive necessity that she had for him. I was an empty likeness of him. My mother assigned something to him and nothing to me. Unconsciously.

When my brother died, the existence in which we had so blindly believed died with him. My brother died and I lived. That was, the true image died, yet the false image remained. I could stand in front of the mirror, but there would be no reflection. My brother was no longer on the other side. All that was left were words. Words describing him, words that remained inscribed in my heart. My brother was real. For my mother, he was real, while I was fake. My brother was the center. The center of the family. My mother and I were cogs gyrating with love around him. My brother was fullness. Fullness that kept the center from feeling empty. Existence itself, a man who firmly accepted our love, who monopolized it for himself. Proof that there was something there. We didn't doubt it.

Words describing my brother appear one after another, disappearing like smoke. They rise up, indefinitely. Like images in a mirror. And then I forget them. I don't remember anything anymore. What was my brother? I don't know. What am I?

A river. A river of words. Words describing my brother rise up coolly, while my real brother is swept away. Beyond that river is the sea of the world. Everything that has been swept away by the river of words. People's pasts. Men and women. My brother disappears into the flow, and everything else follows after him. Like pulling on a corner of a sheet, and causing the entire set of bedding to collapse. Words describing various events. The river flowing through me makes me loquacious, renders me mute. At times, I stare into it, and ramble on without end. I give form to everything flowing through it. But at other times, I fall silent. Pessimistic at the flow of words that refuse to settle, wondering whether I can truly express anything at all.

It is the sun that illuminates the river. Things that can't be seen directly. Its black rays. The sorrow of my brother, of the world, endlessly flowing. A pall falls over me. I can't even bring myself to cry. There is no madness, no hallucination, no violence. Just a vague sense of melancholy. I can't look directly into that blinding blackness. Words. Flowing out of reach. Emotions. A light that can't be looked on directly. Everything that was necessary for life is repudiated before me. I try to think. About what to say while I bear this river, this light. About whom to love. But I talk, and I love. Death and madness are out of the question. Cowardice is my daily life. My everyday life is incoherent. I say things that I never thought that I would say. I confess my feelings to myself, whom I don't at all like. Every day is an opera. A nonsensical fantasy.

Sometimes, I dive into the sheets. Afraid. Afraid that one day, I will regret my everyday life. That I will despise myself for living my life like an opera. Someone sees me. A figure filled with kindness. They worry about me. They touch me through the sheets. And I want to hurt them.

After taking a shower, the youth returned from the bathroom, immaculate. He showed the woman his white skin, steamed like a pork dumpling. He sat on the bed, naked, letting his skin dry. His legs dangling uselessly. He stared into the distance. His skin was dotted with what looked like insect bites and red chilblains. Those marks were all caused by his atopy, he said. Several different diseases, each with the same name, marred his white skin. His skin was chaotic. But his eyes were firm, clear. His head was empty, as revealed by the unconscious swaying of his feet. But those eyes staring into the distance seemed to be filled with intelligence and purpose. Those eyes overwhelmed the chaos of his skin. As though they alone were his essence. Eventually, he turned those wise eyes to the woman. The woman averted her gaze. What? she asked. You're hungry, aren't you? the youth smiled.

The two went to a restaurant on the Hamamachi shopping street. They ordered two glasses of wine, and separate seafood marinades. The woman gulped down her glass of chilled white wine. As she finished, she came back to her senses, and looked at the youth. The youth was sniffing his clothes.

What's wrong? the woman asked.

Do I still smell like frankincense? the youth said.

You do, the woman lied.

Even after making love with you so much? the youth asked. Shouldn't I smell like you by now?

I suppose you're right, the woman sighed. I suppose my scent must have left you when you took a shower.

Then why don't I smell like soap right now?

Well, you *do* smell like soap.

Before, you said I smelled like frankincense.

I was mistaken. You smell like soap.

The youth fell silent. The woman didn't explain. She quietly poured the cool wine down her throat.

Are you trying to steal my scent?

Steal? Would it be that bad?

Yes. It's very bad, stealing someone's scent.

The woman drank her wine with a sense of clarity.

Her husband had given her that perfume. In truth, she didn't really care how she smelled. She was even more indifferent to the idea of possessing a special scent, different from those of everyone else. She had always been that way. Neither she nor the youth was interested in being special. That should have gone without saying.

I like your scent, but I can't steal it. What should I do?

I know a perfume that would suit you more. It's much better than this one. Do you want to try it?

Of course I do.

The youth had no desire to choose his own perfume. The woman had suspected as much.

No matter what it smells like?

Please don't give me anything that smells like frankincense. The youth's expression was one of innocence.

Without responding to that plea, the woman took a sip of her wine. It's the most popular perfume available. It will suit you. I recommend it.

The youth smiled. Of course.

The woman stared into the wine glimmering in her glass. The alcohol stung her eyes. She gave the youth a cynical look. She thought. About being unique. About how she herself had been robbed of all such interest. About her unhappiness. But the youth was different. He didn't think of himself as unhappy. Perhaps he didn't think of himself as happy either. She wondered whether that meant that he had never thought about such things. About whether he was happy or unhappy. About his indifference to being unique. No, he probably hadn't. He was different from her. They may have shared the same indifference, but they were different people.

You're a strange one, aren't you? the woman murmured. It's a lot more attractive to have your own scent. You're better off looking for your own unique scent. Not just buying some popular perfume.

Oh, is that so? So what did you mean a moment ago? Were you just playing with me? Or were you being sarcastic?

Both. Seeing how ignorant you are of scents, I thought the most ordinary perfume around would suit you.

But it has to be better than frankincense, the youth said in all seriousness. And you're right. I don't know anything. So I want the most ordinary one there is.

You would still choose ordinary even if you did know better, the woman murmured.

According to Serge Bolshakoff's *Russian Mystics*, there were a great many saints at the time of Ivan the Terrible known now as *yurodivy*. These fools for Christ, or Holy Fools, would abandon their properties, their homes, their families, and live solely for prayer. Saint Francis of Assisi and Saint Benedict, both famous in the West, are also considered *yurodivy*.

The Byzantine Church has two canonized *yurodivy*, Saint Simeon and Saint Andrew, but there are a great many more in Russia, with four canonized *yurodivy* from the fourteenth century, eleven from the fifteenth century, and seven each from the sixteenth and seventeenth centuries. However, those *yurodivy* didn't leave any writings, and few details are known of their lives.

Adherents of the Orthodox faith pray to Saint Andrew of Constantinople, a righteous Holy Fool who, according to the hagiographies, saw the Theotokos appear on the day after the Feast of the Intercession. Andrew thought not of the riches of this world. He slept out in the open, with no possessions to call his own. Whenever someone mistook him for a beggar, offering him something as an act of charity, he would distribute it instead to the poor. People called him a fool, threatened him, scolded him, encouraged him. The wealthy forbade him to enter their homes, and even the beggars refused to join him.

In order to cultivate their humility, these Holy Fools were willing to undergo not only physical deprivation, but humiliation too.

Dostoevsky's *The Idiot*. The word *idiot* is said to be a reference to *yurodivy*. It appears that at least one such *yurodivy* always appears in each of his works. For example, in *Crime and Punishment*, a man going by the name of Nikolai confesses to Raskolnikov's crimes. The pretrial judge Porfiry is struck with wild inspiration at this. In *Demons*, the beggar-like monk Tikhon is looked upon as though a saint. In the end, even Stavrogin confesses his sins, but Tikhon sees through the arrogance that lies dormant within him.

There is only one icon of a Holy Fool in the Tokyo Holy Resurrection Cathedral. Saint Alexius. That is the name given on the old diagram explaining the icons. However, it seems that identifying a saint as a Holy Fool is a matter of great circumspection. In a later church bulletin, it was explained that he was a Venerable, a saint who had endured severe asceticism. It is difficult to differentiate the two, as both must engage in long, rigorous asceticism, but where the Holy Fool differs from the Venerable lies in their sense of humility. Whether a fatalist or a miracle worker, an arrogant individual is unlikely to be canonized.

Maliciousness welled up in the woman's unconsciousness. The forgiveness of a Holy Fool. She wanted to ascertain its aesthetic value.

In the town of Sarov dwelled one of the most popular saints in all Russia. Today, he is the patron saint to a great many individuals. If you were to speak that name to any Russian, he would be the individual that first comes to mind.

The Sarov Monastery was located on the border of the Nizhny Novgorod and Tambov Governorates in Imperial Russia. It was first constructed in the year 1280, but later deserted due to war, until in 1706, an ascetic known as Ioan arrived, and established a set of strict rules to guide the monks following him. That was the beginning of the monastery. In 1778, at the age of nineteen, the saint knocked on the door of Sarov Monastery. At the age of twenty-seven, he took his vows and received his monastic name—*one who burns*. He began his seclusion at the age of thirty-four, living in a hut in the woods around six kilometers from the monastery.

In the beginning, he would bring home bread from the monastery on Sundays, but he eventually gave up even this luxury, and began to consume only what vegetables and wild plants that he could find growing around his hut. Even when he did bring home bread, he would give it to the animals that came to his hut. Such acts were witnessed by a great many of his fellow monks. The picture of him sharing food with the bears became so famous that for fifteen years, hunters were prohibited from killing bears in the Sarov Forest in commemoration of the saint.

When he died, a chapel was built on his tomb, adorned with an icon of him giving food to the bears, along with two other icons.

People in Russia were so afraid of bears that they forgot their original name for them. Could it be that this fear of bears has played a role in the saint's enduring popularity?

The youth stepped out from the shower. As usual, he lay face-down, naked on the woman's bed to dry off. The woman snuck up on him, spraying a vial of perfume at the nape of his neck. Surprised, he placed his hand over his neck. He glanced around at her.

It's cold, he said. You startled me.

That was my perfume. They don't sell any of the popular men's perfumes here, so I used mine. You like women's scents more anyway, don't you?

That's right. I wonder why something so formless as perfume has to be divided into male and female.

I'll put it on you, the woman said, approaching him.

The youth rubbed his eyes as she sprayed it on his shoulders. It soaks right in, he said.

Those who are accustomed to degrading others can identify the weak by smell. The youth would undoubtedly suffer all manner of degradations in the future. The woman gave him the scent of the weak. The youth was happy. He transferred the scent from his shoulder to the palm of his hand, sniffing it. It smells good, he said. Usually, when someone suffers humiliation, they go mad with hatred. Even after it is all over, and they are faced with one peaceful day after another, still they can't help but recall that experience from time to time. The recollection would be agonizing. Lonely. They would be met by the temptation of death. But would this youth ever forget? How could he wear the same perfume as the woman who had violated him? That perfume was no different from the earrings worn by Egyptian slaves. A means of branding the weak. Maybe he didn't feel that way? But the woman did. You smell just like me, she said. I'm glad, the youth responded. As though they were a pair of lovers. No, as though they were something even more similar. As though their similarity would continue indefinitely. As though the day of separation would never come.

The woman insulted the youth on purpose. She felt irritation toward him, sensitive as he was to such insults. The youth applied his ointment to his body. He hummed to himself. He seemed to be in a good mood now that he had his own scent. The woman began to despise him. You can't cure that disease with medicine, she wanted to say. No matter how much cream you put on it, you'll just scratch at it again.

What's wrong? the youth called out all of a sudden. Were you thinking about something?

Nothing. The woman looked away. Let me rub your medicine on your back. She turned the youth over.

I was wondering, do you have time tomorrow night? Say at around five o'clock? The woman invited the youth out on a date. Five o'clock? That's a little early for dinner, the youth responded. Not for dinner. . . There's somewhere I want to go. Haven't you already been everywhere around Urakami? I want to go to Mount Inasa. Together, you mean? To see the night skyline?

Yes, the woman answered. We'll go on a date.

A date? The youth sank deep into thought. Put simply, he didn't seem pleased by her invitation. The woman stared at him, as though waiting for a verdict. She imagined that he had his own plans, and would decline her offer. If that happened, would she feel upset? Would she cry? Would she be the kind of woman who exploded with emotion? In the end, would she force him to promise to accompany her? No, she wasn't strong enough to do any of that. She would despair, she would descend into sorrow, and spend the time alone. It was as though somewhere, deep in her heart, she was already hoping that the date wouldn't come to fruition. All that she wanted was a fluctuation of emotion. A misty rain to moisten her thirsty womb. If going on a date could grant her that, that was fine. But if she could get it without going on a date, she didn't mind that either. Would this youth be able to move her heart? How much selfishness would he be able to give her, she who had always been at the mercy of men?

Tears, anger, sadness. Sanity had never brought her those

things. The woman had never cried at a funeral. Not even the funeral of the person whom she had loved most. She didn't understand what it meant to cry, even when she had every reason to do so. The only thing that she could understand was that the man, he whom she had once loved, had cried for no reason. That he wasn't in his right mind. He cried for no reason, and when he felt better, he would go back to sleep. Then, he would be reborn as a thirsty man. Now that she thought about it, she realized that crying, for him, had been a means of keeping death at bay. Tears, sleep, rebirth. The cycle repeated itself. When finally he stopped crying, when the people around him said that he was better, that was when he—

What are you thinking? The youth stared into the woman's eyes. What about you? the woman asked him back. Do *you* have any plans? No, nothing in particular, the youth answered. But you can't go out tomorrow, can you? That's what you're thinking, isn't it?

No, it isn't. The youth laughed. I was wondering whether we should take the ropeway or the skyway cable car. I'm looking forward to it.

The youth opened his guidebook.

The ropeway took five minutes to climb from the foot of Mount Inasa to the summit. The skyway reached the summit in half that time, but required passengers to take a taxi partway up the mountain. That night, the woman told the youth that she wasn't interested in the view from the ropeway, and wanted instead to take the skyway. I'm not interested in the scenery, she said. I want to see the couples gathering on the observation deck. The couples? I suppose it must be quite atmospheric up there. They'll probably be quite moved by it. Arm in arm, hugging one another. The youth spoke as though none of this concerned him, as though he had given up on the woman entirely.

There was no one else at the skyway platform. The woman didn't know if that was because of the time of year or whether most visitors normally took the ropeway. They rode the gondola alone. They didn't speak to one another. They merely stared out at the scenery. But there was nothing outside. The skyway didn't share the beautiful night view for which the ropeway was famous. There were a great many deer roaming the mountain. The woman wondered whether the mountainside wasn't some kind of nature park. But neither of them spoke to the other.

The woman looked at the youth. He was staring intently through the window. When he spotted a deer, his face lit up in a faint smile.

How about some sweets? The woman broke the silence, handing the youth a chocolate. Thank you, he said, accepting it. He was holding back laughter. What is it? the woman asked. You're surprisingly straightforward, the youth answered. You probably saw the deer and thought of offering me some chocolate, right? But what you really want to do is go feed the deer, not me.

I wonder, the woman murmured. She was in no hurry to admit that the youth had seen through her, that he had read her heart. He wasn't wrong. It's no laughing matter, she said in exasperation. You think I'm feeding you like an animal, don't you? That *is* kind of unpleasant, the youth murmured, his expression clouding over. Wasn't that what you were saying? the woman asked. I didn't think of it like that, the youth said. I just thought it was funny, imagining you wanting to feed the deer. That's why I laughed. I didn't think you were making fun of me.

The woman sighed.

At the summit, the two of them took the elevator to the top of the observatory. There were several couples there, along with a number of tourists. Here are those couples you were looking for, the youth murmured happily. Thank goodness. He honestly thought that she had come simply to see them.

They stood at the edge of the observatory. The night view sure is beautiful, don't you think? Shall we take a photo? the youth offered. No, the woman refused. No photos. One of the tourists was glancing around, trying to determine in which direction Tokyo lay. The youth followed suit, also looking toward Tokyo.

The woman leaned forward, glancing underneath. They were high enough up that she would surely die if she were to jump. One couple was taking a photograph against the backdrop of the night view. The woman looked down. She felt excited for some reason. The couples seemed happy. Elderly ladies enjoying their lives. The woman couldn't help but let herself feel happy too. She smiled faintly, leaning forward.

All of a sudden, she was pulled forcefully back. The youth had grabbed her arm. That's dangerous, he murmured. His expression was reserved and unnatural. He didn't let go of her arm. His nails dug into her skin. A child was running across the observation platform. Begging his parents to let him look through the telescope. The woman was terrified of the youth.

I understand. I won't go to the edge, so let go of me now. It hurts. A look of deep sorrow fell across the youth's face. He smiled childishly, as though trying to banish that feeling. There's a telescope. Do you want to take a look? he suggested. The woman rejected that idea. I'll take a look, the youth said, putting a coin into the machine. Wow, look how far you can see, he murmured.

The woman rolled up her sleeve, and looked at her arm. The marks left by the youth's fingers were still bright red. Had he noticed that the shadow of death had fallen across her mind? He had reached out unconsciously. To pull her away from death. The youth too was often tempted by death. The woman knew that. But when it came to others, he always tried to pull them back from it. Powerfully. Instinctively. He was a fool. He didn't realize that the woman was ridiculing him. But he had noticed her shadow of death. Strong arms. She had never before felt such a strong resistance to death. From where did this power of resistance arise? Prohibition? Love?

Suddenly, the woman realized that there was a stairwell on the observation platform. It seemed that to leave, one could take the stairs instead of the elevator. The youth possessed an incredible power to steer her away from death. The woman descended the stairs. Could she resist that power? So she wondered.

When the woman returned to her room, she sat down on her bed, and let out a sigh. She had come back alone. Leaving the youth behind. Would he think that she had jumped? She pondered that question for a moment, before deciding that it was unlikely. If someone had leaped from the observation platform, there would have been an uproar. Perhaps he hadn't even realized that she was gone. His eyes might still be fixed to the telescope. Then, as people slowly began to disappear from the observation platform one by one, he would finally realize that he was alone. That he had been left behind. One way or another, he would no doubt return to her room. The woman mused. Would he cry when he realized that he had been left behind? Or would that normally calm and level-headed young man become suddenly enraged? The woman fell back onto the bed in a limp heap. She had hurt someone. She had inflicted pain. It was so physical. The woman had endured harm at the hands of others before. But she had little experience of inflicting harm herself. It was almost impossible for her to do so intentionally. The youth, though sympathizing with her suffering, hadn't surrendered himself to despair. The woman found that strange. When she realized the nature of his reaction, she wanted to make him cry, or else push him toward anger. Love, flesh, desire. Those things no longer existed within her. She was driven by a vague desire to degrade the youth, in a place unrelated to such ambiguous concepts.

There are certain men and women for whom the act of insulting one another serves as a means to enrich their mutual love. Just how removed was the woman, as she was now, from such people? They remained unchanged. From the moment that she had met the youth, the two of them remained unchanged. What existed between them was similarity. Not sexual love. Nonetheless, theirs wasn't an inorganic relationship either. Insofar as they resembled one another, they were like two overlapping rings representing mathematical sets. Or twins who shared a mysterious fate. In the case of the woman and the youth, it went like this. When the woman peered into clear water, she saw the youth. The two of them placed their bodies atop one another countless times. In short, the woman wanted to become one with the youth, and so tried to throw herself into that water. The temptation of death crept up on them, naturally, in a form that neither of them could recognize. Like a ball rolling down a slope. They were being propelled forward by gravity, with death lying in wait up ahead.

But the woman and the youth weren't identical. There was no realm of death beyond the surface of the water. The woman began to realize. What exactly she had done to the youth. It had been like throwing a stone into the surface of the water, into the figure of the youth reflected in it. All to confirm the depth of that water. The fullness of that image. The nature of its being. Was it a false image, or a true one?

The woman rubbed her arms. They were numb. The youth's powerful arms. The strength of his crushing grip around her. A night view that stretched as far as the eye could see. Three hundred and sixty degrees of neon lights, ports, ships. The lights were small, but they were certain, steady. The woman was struck with vertigo. The vertigo of life. Her head spun as some great force pulled her out from the world of death and up into the world of life. Like a deep-sea fish being pulled up to the surface, and bursting because it couldn't withstand the change in pressure. She felt a sense of danger. The woman pondered. That some part of her had judged the youth to be incompetent. She had assumed that his grip would be just as weak as his attitude toward her, as his appearance. But that grip had the power to affirm life. And the power to force others to do the same. She found it frightening. If he were a normal, healthy man, he wouldn't have cared whether she lived or died. He would think only that if he were living an honest, decent life, so too must this careless, undisciplined woman.

The urge to die. The urge to live. It was like having a seizure, like being possessed. The woman sensed that the youth had suffered mistreatment at the hands of others. People found all sorts of reasons and opportunities to persecute those around them. At some cognitive level, he might even want to die. But when faced with death, he rebelled against it. Forcefully. The unexpected strength of his grip on her arm struck her as a mystical force. The expression that had fallen over his countenance for a brief moment. As though to admonish her. So stern, as though he had broken one of the commandments and wanted to plunge himself into the depths of hell. That weak-minded youth. The person who had felt compassion for her. Surely he couldn't understand? Why he had rescued her from death. Or even why he had affirmed life. It was a kind of madness. A madness for life. He had been driven by that madness to keep on living, right up to the present moment. No matter the mistreatment that he suffered. The woman realized. That they would never be able to understand each other. No matter how long they spoke in unison about their suffering, he would always stand between her and death. He would push her away from any attempt to comfortably become one with him, and force her to face life as an independent being. He had already done so. He had confronted her on that path to death, and stopped her.

The night deepened. Yet the youth didn't come to the woman's room. She was resolved. For him to wail that she had left without telling him, for him to rail at her, for him to say that he had been worried for her safety. She envisioned a wide assortment of attitudes that he might take. Yet he didn't so much as reveal himself. The woman lay down on the bed. She decided to try falling asleep. She would undoubtedly see him tomorrow, one way or another. She closed her eyes, but she couldn't drift off. She had no choice. She would need a drink to help her sleep. There was a twenty-four-hour convenience store nearby. She decided to go there.

She took the elevator down to the lobby. The youth was picking up his room key at the front desk. The woman felt as though she had just spotted a famous movie actor on the television. She couldn't tell if he was real or not. Her heart stood still. She wasn't surprised. She merely blinked in puzzlement. The youth's sudden appearance was almost difficult for her to accept. He noticed her. He raised his hand to signal her. He smiled. The resolution that she had steeled in herself evaporated. The woman didn't respond.

Are you going somewhere? the youth asked. The woman nodded, weakly. Good night, he said, pushing the button for the elevator. The youth turned his back on her, and waited for the elevator doors to open. The woman stared at his back. The elevator arrived. The sound of the doors opening. The youth turned to her. Um, he said. For the first time, the woman's heart began to beat. The pounding intensified. She widened her eyes. To show that she had heard him. There's a vending machine here at the hotel, if you want a drink, the youth said.

The woman and the youth bought some beer. They went to

the youth's room. Since they had bought the beer together, they would drink it together too. Without a pretext like that, they wouldn't be able to meet. There wouldn't be anything to say.

You came back first, didn't you? the youth said as he pulled back the tab on his can of beer. Yes, the woman answered. You're back late. I am, the youth continued. I kept looking for you, until I realized you must have left without me. By the time I thought of coming back myself, the ropeway had finished for the day. So I called a taxi and had it come up to the top of the mountain. That's why I'm so late. I see. The woman didn't apologize.

Suddenly, the youth stared straight into the woman, his expression stern. The woman ignored him. She poured her beer down her throat. She pretended to be thirsty. Did you go down the mountain by yourself? the youth asked. Yes, the woman answered cheerfully. She wiped the foam from her lips. A woman taking the ropeway down the mountain by herself. . . It pains my heart just thinking about it. The youth stared downward, his shoulders slumping in an exaggerated gesture. The woman laughed. It's nothing compared to how lonely *you* must have been. You waited up there alone until the taxi arrived, right? I'm fine, the youth said. That was my own fault. *I'm* the one who left without saying anything, the woman said. But if I hadn't been preoccupied with the telescope, you wouldn't have lost your patience, the youth continued. I was messing around by myself. I thought it would be fun to look for the harbor together, or to work out which direction Tokyo was. I'm not interested in the port, or in Tokyo either, the woman answered.

More importantly, she continued, I was going to die. You stopped me.

You were going to die? The youth's face blanched. I guess that isn't too surprising, given how much you're dealing with.

You look like you've only just realized it. That I was thinking of dying up there.

This *is* the first I've heard about you dying on that mountain, the youth answered.

That's a lie, the woman murmured, turning pale. You grabbed my arm when I was about to jump. Don't you remember? It hurt. I thought you were going to kill me before I could throw myself over the edge.

I did grab your arm. Because I thought it was dangerous, that you might fall. But I didn't think you were trying to jump on purpose.

But you glared at me, the woman said quietly. As though trying to soothe herself. Like you knew I was going to do something bad.

If you really wanted to do something bad, I wouldn't be able to stop you. I'm too weak, too timid.

But you did, the woman said, frightened. You did.

I see. The youth let out a sigh of relief. All of a sudden, he flashed her a smile. So that's it. I guess I'm lucky. He hugged the woman. Innocently. Softly. The strength with which he had grabbed her arm was nowhere to be seen. The woman closed her eyes as those arms wrapped around her. Feeling something akin to an unpleasant chill. I'd miss you if you died, the youth murmured.

People lined up, one after the next. On that day, people took turns to have their bodies, their whole bodies, treated with antiseptic solution. But even in the midst of treatment, their thoughts turned to death. Like a dream. Like a goal. Neither the nurses nor the ointment could defy the gravity of death pressing down on them. And there, their thoughts turned to life. So unnaturally. Like consciously standing yourself up on your hands, and walking upside down. Which was why this youth's state of obliviousness should have been impossible.

Hey, the woman called out weakly. You believe in the resurrection of man, don't you? I look for the resurrection of the dead. That's the eleventh part of the Nicene Creed, the youth answered. Tell me the story of the resurrection. The resurrection of Christ? Or the resurrection of Lazarus? I don't mind. You could even make up your own story.

Dear me. The youth began to rummage through his suitcase for his Bible.

In *Crime and Punishment*, there is a scene in which Raskolnikov, after coming to his senses, asks the prostitute Sonya to read him the story of the resurrection of Lazarus. After hearing this passage, Raskolnikov decides to turn himself in for murder. If this were a true story, it would be a major drama. An intelligent young man is converted by a prostitute. The Orthodox Church venerates several saints who were once prostitutes. Saint Mary of Egypt is one such example. Prostitutes. Women demeaned in body and soul. They were never given the good fortune or opportunity to adopt arrogance. They were left with no choice but to follow the harsh, narrow road to humility. If a man who abandons his property and feigns madness is a Holy Fool, a male saint, then a prostitute who adorns the disgraced name of a whore is a holy woman. In the case of *Crime and Punishment*, the situation is even more complicated. Sonya's father, Marmeladov, insists that he is more worthy of sainthood than she is. His argument is as follows. Sonya, who became a prostitute to save her father from poverty, is considered by all as piteous and filial. That is a reasonable analysis. However, Marmeladov argues that he, wracked by guilt after selling his daughter into prostitution, who can do no more than drink himself to ruin, is more worthy of being considered a saint than she is. A good many people sympathize with this argument. However, to argue this is to change the definition of sainthood. The conventional image of a saint, such as those found in typical Catholic hagiographies like the *Legenda Aurea*, is of an individual who performs miracles or heals the sick. However, when we consider the large number of Holy Fools in Russia, the close affinity between prostitutes and saints, and Marmeladov's argument in *Crime and Punishment*, we realize that miracles and healing are less important to the Russian idea of sanctity. Rather, sainthood seems to be measured by the degree to which one is demeaned. These people take their humiliation in stride. Masochism works in an emasculated realm divorced from sexual love. Indeed, this idea is especially dangerous to the general public. The number of saints canonized as *yurodivy* in Russia has dropped over the years. Even the saint of Sarov recognized the danger of knowing them too deeply, of practicing their form of asceticism.

Crime and Punishment is widely considered to be a story that dismisses the idea of sexual love. In Dostoevsky's creative notes, there is a description of an omitted scene in which Raskolnikov and Sonya become romantically involved. Did the author think that it would be improper for his protagonist to have a romantic relationship with a holy prostitute?

I lived my brother's existence as though it were my own. After he died, I lived with the absence of the self. The absence of my brother was the absence of my sense of self. I thought of myself as unfortunate. But as I grew older, I found myself crying whenever I remembered my brother. I could sympathize with his anguish and madness, with so much. I still do. But I haven't thrown myself off a rooftop like he did. I forget about that family sometimes. I'm so busy with housework and childcare. I'm sure of it. My brother and I share the same anguish, the same madness. They are the same kind, the same scale. But life and death have cut our lives in half. I weep. Over my brother's weakness. Over my own resilience. I notice it.

Clearly. Acutely. My brother on the other side of the mirror looks nothing like me. He is the other. Dissimilar to me. An other with a fullness of being. I am no longer a false image of him. *I* am the other. I am the other to my brother. And I am also a complete being. As the other. An affirmation of my own existence. An affirmation of my self-identity. This realization doesn't particularly make me happy. Nor does it make me unhappy. My brother is dead. My mother is still alive. My mother is destitute, having lost her breadwinner son. She became mentally ill after my brother's death. She became an irresolute spendthrift. I gave her money. Money saved from my own allowance. She broke down into tears, thanking me. But her gratitude lasted only for that brief moment. She spent it immediately. As though she had just come into easy money. After my brother died, things just got worse. But I knew that I would never be stupid enough to do anything that would cause myself to die too. I know that I'm different from my brother. I remember him, sometimes. I have more good memories of him now. But my past is still a mess. My mother lives like a phantom, burdened by the past. But I'm no longer filled with cynicism.

The two of them finished their beers. The woman felt tipsy. Have you had enough? the youth asked. Yes, I'm fine, the woman answered. Really? That's a bit of a surprise. I thought you were the kind of person who likes to drink themselves into a stupor. The woman laughed. That was certainly the case the first day I met you. I had a yorsh. You must know what that is. A yorsh, the youth murmured. You drank beer and vodka together. That's right, the woman said. My father used to drink like that too, the youth answered. He was a heavy drinker. The woman laughed. I thought as much.

You. . . The woman stared at the youth, her eyes glistening. Yes, your mother was Russian. That's right, the youth nodded.

Did you ever go to the Russian Club? The Russian Club? There was a place for Russians to meet at the church, right? They would all get together over tea after the Eucharist.

The Russian Club. The youth raised his voice, as though speaking up into the sky. We never went to the Russian Club. My Japanese father never showed any interest in it. Most of the time, we went straight home after the Eucharist. But when I was young, my father was a representative for the congregation, so we would stay back at the church until late for meetings. But that's all a distant memory now. I was an altar server, so I was always busy.

How did you become an altar server? Was that your father's idea?

I don't remember. Even in my earliest memories, I was already carrying the Metropolitan's crosier. Like it was only natural for me to do so.

I know. That crosier is so heavy, isn't it? Yes, you can't carry it without strength of will. But you didn't need strength of will, did you? I'm all alone now.

Alone? Why? the youth asked. The woman didn't respond.

Back when I attended the church, there was a novice training to become a monk. The novice was responsible for making the sacramental bread. Sacramental bread has to be cooked at a certain humidity. Whenever the windows clouded over in the bakery room, that signified that he was busy preparing it. It was always hot and humid in the bakery room. The novice would wear short sleeves as he set to his task, even in the middle of winter. He let me help him. He let me stamp the seal of the Theotokos on the dough. Eventually, when I couldn't stand the heat anymore, and sat down feeling anemic, he would pull a popsicle from the freezer, and hand it to me. He hid the popsicles in the same place where he froze the bread. This happened several times. Eventually, a member of the congregation heard about this, and I was warned not to enter the bakery room again. Because the novice wanted to become a monk. He wasn't in a position where he could afford to meet a woman behind closed doors.

The woman breathed a sigh. She and the youth were sitting next to each other on the sofa. She leaned against the armrest away from him. She didn't lean on his shoulder. Do you want to lie down? the youth asked. No, the woman answered. This is *your* bed. The youth quickly realized what she meant by those words. Weak-minded people often have a good sense of intuition. You're saying you won't sleep with me anymore, aren't you? he asked. Yes, the woman answered. I understand. But you can still sleep here. You look tired. The youth smiled. He wasn't hurt. He wasn't happy either. Theirs was a relationship that comprised both love and degradation, and so there was no joy or sorrow to be found in ending it. Or perhaps both existed. Now that he understood, the woman leaned against the youth's shoulder. The youth grasped her hand. The woman squeezed his back. The youth blushed. Hah, he laughed softly.

The youth kept on laughing. The woman felt suddenly lonely. She lacked the strength to wound the youth's heart. No matter what she did, she couldn't wound his tough heart. The youth kept on laughing. It made the woman feel lonely. She would never be able to hold him again. Because the two of them weren't identical. By embracing each other, they would no doubt create opposing boundary lines. The woman's memories. Memories of degradation. She could no longer sympathize with the youth. The smell of perfume. She couldn't be sure. Did it belong to her, or to him? But she knew that she and the youth were different people. Even if she couldn't distinguish between them by smell, she could tell the difference from their mutual existences. The memory of degradation was certainly present in the youth. But this youth, this holy prostitute, wasn't tainted by death. He affirmed life. Unconsciously, but powerfully. The woman wanted to cry. She had met a man of flesh and blood in Nagasaki. A living man. Yet she had come here to witness death, to attune herself to it. What was she to make of this? She felt like crying in the face of this cosmic irony. What in the world was this living man doing to her? She began to feel increasingly lonely. She had been thrown into a world devoid even of sympathy. She didn't embrace the youth. His body no longer brought her comfort.

The woman washed the youth's body in the bath. She lathered up the soap in her hands, and rubbed it into his flesh so as not to irritate his skin. The youth laughed. A shriek of laughter, like a child playing in water. The woman, surrendering herself to his joy, laughed with him. This youth was by no means docile. His behavior was more than a little mischievous. More than she could handle. He may have said that he wanted her to clean him, everywhere, but he wasn't about to let her do it. He said that it was unfair that only he was naked. The woman explained that there was no need for her to undress. In the first place, he had inflammations in places that he wouldn't be able to reach by himself, she explained. The purpose of this was for her to wash them for him. Not for them to bathe together. The corners of the youth's lips curled, his eyes narrowing in enjoyment. He looked unconvinced. In a joking way. The woman had a tough time washing away the foam in the shower. The youth showed her his back. As though to dodge a water gun attack. He wouldn't let her wash him off easily. The woman let out a sigh. She dipped the towel into the water, and wiped the rest of his body. What an unreasonable boy you are. The woman pressed the towel against the youth's head, using her fingers to draw a cross. Are you imitating a priest? Using a towel as an epitrachelion stole? Yes, the woman answered. We used to do that a lot when I was a kid, the youth continued.

Fooling around in the sanctuary. Or jumping on the bishop's throne. If you did that now, you would be excommunicated, the woman said.

Once the youth's body was clean, he wandered around the room, naked. As usual, he let his body dry exposed to the air. He wasn't ashamed of his nakedness. He didn't even have the wisdom to hide his genitals. The youth, still unclothed, tried to hug her from behind. The woman told him to stop. Why? the youth asked sadly. I went through all that effort getting you clean, the woman said. You'll get dirty again. And you'll get my clothes wet. She had no trouble persuading him. No matter how transparent the lie. The youth collapsed sprawled onto the bed. As though to say that he was bored. He didn't even dry his hair. The woman found that curious. The youth had beautiful, straight hair. Slightly brown in color. Like under-roasted coffee beans. No hairdryer was necessary to maintain the beauty of that hair. Even without having been dried, those strands were straight, their color unchanging.

The youth wept. He wept because he pitied the woman. Quite as though he blamed himself for her suffering. He thought of himself as helpless. He believed that the only option available to him was to cry. He didn't remember. That he had forced the woman to live. The strength of his grip on the woman's arm. The sternness of his gaze. He didn't realize that there were those parts to himself. The woman understood the beauty of a helpless person's tears, the beauty of someone who had convinced themselves of their own helplessness. She told him that there was no need to cry, that none of it could have been helped. Hearing this, the youth wept all the more. The woman was fascinated by his tears.

The youth asked her to marry him. The woman refused. Why do you have to leave me all alone? the youth asked. The woman didn't answer. It was she who had been left alone.

Eventually, the youth cried himself to exhaustion, and fell asleep. The woman was alone. But the insensitive youth hadn't noticed that. He, who was so fearful of being left in solitude, had instead left her alone. He lay beside her, white as a corpse. The woman wondered whether he might never wake. She could hear him breathing in his sleep. As he was lying on his side, she found herself imagining that it was his ears that were breathing in and out. He turned over in his sleep, without a care in the world. The breath of life brushed against that corpse. Even when he turned in bed, he never put himself in a strange sleeping position. He simply lay on his back. The comforter was undisturbed, hiding everything below his neck.

When he opened his eyes, the woman smiled at him, stroking his hair. The youth stretched. Only now did he act like a living being. He brought the woman's hand to his cheek. The woman asked whether he wanted to eat some sweets. The youth had never refused this offer before. He believed that the number of sweets that she offered was proportional to her love for him. The youth narrowed his eyes with a mature smile. It was an expression that couldn't be faked. The woman's kindness had brought him joy. He had completely forgotten that she hadn't accepted his proposal.

The woman and the youth ate the sweets. The youth forgot about his proposal. They spoke about unrelated topics. His grandmother's dacha in Russia. The sights that they had seen in Nagasaki. The youth offered to give her the souvenirs that he had bought. He no longer tried to ascertain whether or not she liked him. The woman found that curious. But she too soon found herself forgetting. Perhaps she had the youth's kindness to blame for that. Even though she didn't love him, he remained kind to her, as though to return her absent affections. He even offered her one of his leftover sweets.

In the land of Nagasaki, a woman lusts for a man. A dead

man. A corpse scorched by a brilliant flash of light. A corpse that can't even be identified. The woman sighs erotically, panting, pointing at her breasts. This personal folly can only be carried out in the most historical of places. But only now does the woman realize that the object of her desire is an illusion. Does that make her a tragic figure?

Don't use my perfume anymore, the woman said. The youth had just been about to apply it to his skin. He grasped the bottle of perfume tightly, staring at her. He remained perfectly motionless, like a frog. Don't use my perfume anymore, the woman repeated. Why not? The youth tilted his head to one side. He blinked innocently a few times. His face proclaimed his confidence that the woman wouldn't say anything to wound him. Because I don't like it, the woman said dismissively. She had tried, clumsily, to attack him. The youth's expression turned serious. The woman looked away. I'm no good at hurting people. Wanting to hurt someone is completely different than actually doing it. I mean, it isn't like I'm about to lose it, that perfume. It's already mine. The woman turned her back on the youth, and stared out the window. I'll buy you your own. How does that sound? The youth rose to his feet. The woman glanced over her shoulder. The youth placed the bottle of perfume in her palm. He showed her his empty hands. I won't lay a finger on it again. How does that sound? The youth laughed. As though in pain. The woman's heart hurt. It hurt to realize that the youth too hurt. He had realized it. That their similarities were disappearing, one by one. The two of them were now different beings. They could no longer share in one another's suffering, as they had before. They had both realized this, at the exact same moment. The surface of the sorrow that had lapped against their heels was now washing over their heads. They had exposed themselves to that soothing sorrow. To that kind and orderly sorrow. A cyclical sorrow that waxed and waned. The youth embraced the woman. I think you're attractive. The woman snuggled into his chest. I'm filled with cheap words of praise. I'm sure there's a perfume that suits you. Not a mundane perfume. A refined and elegant one. I'm glad, the youth murmured. But those words weren't heartfelt. Like a missing tooth. But there were undeniably traces of past nerves. Of old bloodstains. The woman wanted to please the youth. From the bottom of her heart. To fill him with sorrow. To fill him with joy. The woman's desire wavered between these two poles. The youth was separated now from her body. A complete other. But the woman recognized in his emotions the same bruises that she found in herself. She didn't know how to meet this other. Should she welcome him, or turn away in revulsion?

Even when death might be lurking just around the corner, I have to live in opposition to it. Because I don't know how to live any other way. I remember that when I go to restaurants. I don't drink alcohol at such times. I don't want to toss down alcohol in a toast to someone's health. That day, I bought so much at the liquor store. Pernod, Bénédictine, Strega. The child came with me. This one looks so pretty, he said, pointing to a bottle of Galliano. I bought that too. There wasn't anything in particular that I wanted to drink. If it were possible to drink alcohol in its purest form, I probably would have. I bought more than just liquor. Pâté de foie gras, caviar, salmon, beef jerky, olives, pickles. The child, amused by all this shopping, added a bag of potato chips and a box of chocolates to the basket. I didn't get mad at him. Perhaps I would have, any other day. But not that one. The child was bursting with excitement. He was always in high spirits whenever I prepared to drown myself in drink. He believed that anyone buying so much on impulse had to be in a good mood.

The child wasn't the only one who thought that way. When

I came home with my shopping bags, my husband laughed out loud. You've been busy, he said. I ignored him. Only at times like that do I want to hurt my husband. But my obtuse husband offered to pour for me. He filled a glass with clear Pernod. He added water. The Pernod turned yellow. The child was captivated by that change. Wow, he said.

When I get drunk, I can laugh sloppily. I can hug my child naturally. I can joke with my husband. I consider myself truly fortunate. I have a vague sense of gratitude for something. I want to say thank you. Thank you. Thank you. My brother is at the end of that sentence. I become hopeful. I can remember only positive memories of my brother. You're in a good mood today, my husband said. I considered telling him about my brother. I even felt a sense of love for my mother, forever exploiting me. It was at the height of such happiness that my brother died. Everyone praised him. Everyone was happy because of him. Right, I thought. If I leaped now, I could probably reach the other side of the rainbow. Without resenting anyone. The idea of slamming into cold, hard concrete vanished entirely from my mind. Only if I did it now. But I wouldn't. The child was gnawing on the beef jerky that I had bought. My husband was trying to figure out how to make a cocktail with the Bénédictine. My dying at the height of happiness would only teach them about a world of contradiction that they don't need to know. I don't love myself as my brother had. I couldn't force my selfishness on them. All that I can do is stay optimistic. No matter how difficult things become, I don't share in my brother's suffering anymore. The longer that I live, the more that I will diverge from him.

Morning. The youth didn't come to the restaurant where they usually ate breakfast. The woman bought some sandwiches at a store, and made her way to his room. She sounded the chime, and the door swung open. The youth seemed fine.

Please, he said, inviting her inside. As the woman entered the room, she was greeted by a thick cloud of smoke, along with a familiar scent. What's this smell? And the smoke? Are you burning incense? she asked. It's frankincense. Did you forget? the youth said.

Frankincense, the woman murmured. I thought I knew that scent. Faintly. That scent belongs to the past for me. Why are you burning it?

So I don't need to use your perfume, the youth answered. Instead of using your perfume, I'm making myself smell like frankincense.

But I thought you hated that smell? You don't want a new perfume? I did promise to buy you one.

The youth didn't respond to this. Ah, I'm so hungry, he said, lying down on the bed with his limbs outstretched. The woman offered him a sandwich. The youth accepted it. Thank you, he said. As though his immediate concern was simply food. Feigning ignorance. Not saying anything more about the frankincense.

The youth ate the sandwich with relish. The woman found herself growing impatient. I don't like this smell, she tried saying. Can't you do something about it? I'll buy you a proper perfume.

It *would* be nice, a perfume you picked out for me. The youth said only that, as though his attention were focused somewhere else. He was concentrating on the sandwich. Then he added: When are you leaving Nagasaki?

The thorns of frustration that had been raining down on the woman shattered like crystals on her chest. She came to her senses. The youth was right. Too right. She reminded herself that he wasn't her lover.

And you decided that your scent was frankincense, she murmured, before falling silent.

The youth placed a hand atop the woman's head. I'll put it

out. The smell should be enough by now. His hand on her head was gentle. But not passionate.

I still have this image in my memory. Of my brother stacking all the cushions and chairs from the floor on his bed. I'm cleaning my room, he said. I'm throwing away all the beer cans and liquor bottles. He was busy stuffing them all into a garbage bag. I'm going to stop drinking from today, he vowed. But his sobriety wouldn't last more than a few days. My mother and I both knew that. Nonetheless, seeing him cleaning up, seeing him trying to get sober, brought us joy. The cat strolled into his room. No doubt it was wondering what was going on. The cat clambered to the very top of the pile, bed to chair to cushion, and sat itself down. It wanted to show us all that it was the most important member of this household. My brother rested his hands against his hips for a moment, before chasing it off with a broom. The cat was so startled that it leaped off the cushion, knocking it down to the floor. My mother and I laughed. We rarely laughed. But that was why we could be so amused by such a trivial sight.

After we finished cleaning, my mother suggested that we go out to eat. She could be incredibly generous at times like this. She suggested that we go to a bistro in town. Though we didn't have any money, she told us to eat whatever we wanted. But no alcohol allowed. Because today was a celebration. A day to commemorate my brother's sobriety. We had a full meal at the bistro. We congratulated my brother over a toast of Perrier. My mother led the toast. Here's to sobriety, she said. How many times had I raised a glass to my brother's sobriety? But on this particular day, we couldn't help but enjoy ourselves. We laughed like idiots. I've had enough of the psych ward, my brother said. They lock me in my room. They won't even let me go out for a jog. It's just Uno and poker, all day long. We all laughed at this. As though we were all drunk. My brother said that he wanted to find a job as soon as possible. That he wanted to help improve things for the family. He took my mother's hand, and raised it into the air. What's with this shabby ring? I'll earn enough money to buy you a better one. My mother was so moved that tears streamed down her face. We had heard this proclamation many times over. I'll work, I'll make life easier for you, I'll buy you a ring. Yet no matter how many times my mother heard such promises, she never grew tired of them. She cried every time. Every single time that she heard him say them. I too was so excited that I gulped down my glass of Perrier. The carbonated liquid burst in my mouth. The blurred outlines of my family began to acquire fresh definition. My poor but generous mother. My decent, kind-hearted brother. I loved them both. Whenever my brother was sane, the family was all right. My brother had the power to clarify vague perceptions. It didn't matter whether he did so for the right reasons. Because I didn't have the ability to judge those reasons in the first place.

The woman and the youth decided to pay a visit to Ōura Church. The youth suggested that they buy some souvenirs, as they would both be leaving this land soon. The woman agreed. Readily.

There were a great many souvenir shops on the slope leading up to Ōura Church. The woman and the youth shared a parasol as they climbed the slope. They rummaged through the souvenirs on display. A child in a school uniform, probably on a class trip, was drinking a juice, a local specialty flavor. The woman's lips curled in a smile as she watched the child. She smiled when she saw the other children too. Because she was a mother. Her heart was still. The young man noticed the woman's faint smile. Do you like children? he asked. Yes, I do. . .a little, the woman answered. It isn't like I don't like kids, but it's painful for me seeing them at that age, the youth said.

Why? the woman asked. I don't have any good memories of my student days. I didn't have many friends, I was lonely, and I was no good when it came to studying Russian or Japanese. Or English too, for that matter. I knew you were that kind of student, the woman said. I thought as much, the youth remarked. I was sure you would have realized. That I was that sort of kid. The youth rested a hand on the woman's shoulder. They remained silent for a while. Thinking different thoughts. Thoughts too trivial to put into words.

The woman spotted a store filled with stuffed toys. She wondered whether she should buy one for her child. After all, he was still little, and probably wouldn't want anything unique to Nagasaki. He would probably prefer the kind of toy that could be found in any corner of the world. The woman tried to picture it. Her child rejecting something that she had bought for him. I don't want it, he might say. I don't need it. That what he desired, what he wanted, would be beyond her capacity for imagination. The child's desires would be outside her reach. For the first time, the woman understood the reality of his existence. It had taken her a long time to realize this. So very long. The woman remembered. There was a time when even the difference between her own consciousness and that of the child had been unclear. Before she had sympathized with this youth, before he had replaced her, before she had visited this land. To the woman, it seemed like such a long time ago. She and the youth weren't connected. Not in mind, not in body, not in place. It had been the same when they had first met. She simply hadn't realized it. The woman pictured it. A child cut off from herself. A child whose thoughts were different from hers, whose desires were different from hers. She couldn't make that child happy. It had been that way for as long as she could remember.

One of the children, a girl, was having a tantrum. She resembled the man whom the woman had loved. And she resembled the woman herself. The child's kindergarten teacher often complained to the woman. Your son keeps stealing from his friends. When everyone asks him to give them their things back, he hits them. He says they belong to him. At times, the woman would laugh with wild delight, while at others she would flash the teacher a wan smile. Once, she even said to the teacher that her child's mystical behavior was the result of divine inspiration. Now, she felt pity for her son, having to suffer a mother who would say such things.

My mother and I never saw my brother's body. The police wouldn't let us. They insisted that the sight was too tragic and gruesome to witness. He had jumped from such a high place. There was no denying that it must have been tragic. I imagined an egg slipping out of my hand. My mother and I didn't know much about death. It was too tragic to comprehend. For my mother, even the death of her son was a good memory. She loved him too much. He took his shoes off, he lined them up so neatly, and he leaped off the roof like he was jumping into a swimming pool, his hands like this. My mother put her fingers together, as though in prayer. She spoke as though she herself had seen him jump. After my brother died, my mother become kinder to me. Calmer. Gentler. She only remembered good things. She had always been hard on me when my brother was alive, as though to make up for all her doting on him. Sometimes, she would talk about him in recollection. She would presume to speak for his feelings. He wanted us to live together, the three of us, you, your brother, and me, forever, she said. As though she hadn't even considered the possibility that I might one day get married. But I let her be. Because my mother was simply doting on my absent brother. Because that was her way of stealing a momentary glimpse of freedom from the vague sense of malice and anger that otherwise possessed her. A great deal of time had passed since I had experienced the horror of my mother identifying with my brother. Thanks to that, my mother had treated my brother and me in very different ways. But my brother is gone now. And I've learned to endure the way that my mother treats me. Now, I can see her only as a burst of transparent light.

Faces. Faces. Faces. In the midst of all those burnt-out fields, everyone has the same face. Strictly speaking, there are no faces at all. They have all lost their faces to grief. The same is true for the woman. She has no face. Then, a youth, the only person with a face, looks at her. The woman begins to cry. Her tears are an insult. Tears can't express the tragedy of six thousand degrees. Yet still she can't help but cry.

The woman and the youth walked up the slope. A large, black, gaunt stray dog approached them. Its appearance was like a huge shadow. The dog sniffed the youth. It wagged its tail. It liked him. It began to rub its large body against him. The youth stepped back. His expression was one of joy. The dog reared up, and braced its front paws against the youth. The passersby watched on, smiling. The youth too broke into an embarrassed grin. He retrieved a piece of bread from his backpack, probably a leftover from breakfast, and gave it to the dog.

The woman watched on from a distance. With a superficial smile, just like those of the people around her. She became one with the crowd. To the youth, she wasn't special. The dog devoured the bread in the youth's hand. That hand was practically being consumed whole by the dog's mouth. It was probably just a trick of the eyes, but the hand seemed to the woman no different from the bread itself. The dog was consuming the youth with relish. It was eating the thing that had groped the woman's body. The thing that had grabbed her breasts, that had sunken deep into her vagina. The woman thought. That she had eaten it too. What that dog was eating now. She came to a realization. That the youth's hand touched all things equally. She stared at it. The youth's face. His stern countenance. The face of a shepherd. The dog consumed the youth with relish. Such an innocent creature. Judging by its expression, it hadn't realized. That the youth was offering himself, as sustenance. The dog was undoubtedly engrossed in the youth. It wouldn't be content to consume anything else, no matter how fine. It would starve for the rest of its life. Longing for the taste of the youth. Yearning to consume him again. The woman, who herself had consumed the youth, could never be as innocent as the dog was now. She couldn't forget the stern cast of the youth's face. The youth could fill her stomach, or starve her to death. Either course of action would be trivial for him. The woman felt suddenly afraid of the youth. She wanted to hide somewhere where he couldn't see her. Somewhere in the shadows, somewhere where the sun's light wouldn't reach. She glanced around. She could see countless beggars. Help me, give me food. The beggars clung to the youth. To devour him. The youth didn't move a muscle. He remained still, his legs as firm as stone. What kind of countenance did he possess now? He turned toward the woman. But his face was silhouetted by a ring of light.

Matushka Lyubov. The wife of the youngest deacon. She would always gather guests at the clergy house for parties. Both on weekdays and on Sundays. On weekdays, she would invite her friends. On Sundays, she would have members of the congregation over for tea. She always invited a great many guests. I had never seen the Matushka alone with anyone. She would always be the center of a large group. She held those parties of hers seemingly every day. But no one in the congregation was particularly close to her. Nor was the Matushka particularly close to anyone else. She had no hobbies. She no longer played the piano, which had been her sole hobby. In the Church, the piano was considered a vulgar pastime. Housework, prayer, and parties. That was the Matushka's life. During those parties, the Matushka wouldn't utter so much as a word. Everyone else would talk for as long as they pleased. They would forget that she was the one who had organized the party in the first place. They would forget even that the Matushka herself was still present. For example, when the congregation members gathered, they might discuss how to make the singing of the hymns more beautiful. They would say all kinds of things, making full use of their musical knowledge. But the Matushka wouldn't say anything. She would sit there, pale, staring into her cup of tea. No one in the congregation knew that she had graduated from a music college. One of her guests would say something about music, something clearly mistaken. No one else in the congregation would pick up on it. The Matushka did. Yet she said nothing. I attended one of those parties. A member of the congregation invited me. They told me simply that I could eat and drink, for free. When I entered the clergy house, I found that so many members of the congregation were indeed eating and drinking and discussing the liturgies. But my mind was blank. I was mesmerized by the Matushka's ashen solitude.

On the day of the Divine Liturgy, the Matushka snuck timidly into the cathedral. She was carrying a great many candles in her hand. Ten in total. She was especially fervent in her prayers to the icon of Pantaleon, the saint of medicine. For whom was she praying? Was there someone whom she wanted to be healed? The Metropolitan entered the hall, and began to recite the scripture. The congregation began to move. People lined up in front of the analogion to repent, the choir, having finished practice, assembled with their music sheets in the hall, and people took their seats on the pews. The Matushka remained motionless. She was staring straight at the icon. Her lips white. She wasn't wearing any makeup. Her appearance was sickly. But she didn't run away, as though she were already trapped in the cathedral. She was confronting the iconostasis. I decided to confirm her sanity. I let out a small shriek. It was the first time that I had ever felt like screaming while watching someone in their right mind.

It was so sudden. Before I knew it, I could put everything about my family, about my brother, my mother, and myself, into words. That period of my life in which I had been unable to give order to the things coursing through my head had passed. I had returned to sanity. Out of nowhere, I was hit by that sudden realization. Like a tall cedar tree struck by lightning and split instantly into two. I could put it into words. That family that, in my confusion, I had thought impossible to give form. Clumsily. With a distinct, peculiar rhythm. They certainly weren't faithful, those words. But I could live with that. Disloyalty to fidelity is proof of sanity. Now that I could put it into words, there was no one left. No brother or mother around me. The two of them were no more than the liquid that dyed the long plumage of my story. My brother, my mother, and me. A grotesque community not worthy of any symbol. We hadn't been completely independent, but nor had we been identical. It had been horrifying. But I can't remember it anymore. Not that horror, not its raw details. I can speak only of memories. Of superficial things. The words come easily. I can't touch on those three grotesque selves, their essences. There is no essence to my words. Only fragmentary memories. No timeline. There is a book in my mind, its pages in disarray. I don't know my own ending yet. Is it the death of my brother? My life with my healthy and good husband? Or is it even further into the future? I don't know what the truth is. Nor do I have the will to decide it for myself. I have no opinions. I can't decide the center of my own story. I watch my own story from the outside, like a spectator. Remarking that it seems indifferent to persuasion. Wondering who the author is.

I once saw my brother engrossed in reading. He was in the midst of a terrible drinking binge. For those few brief days, it was as though a light had been shone on his life. He forgot all about drink, and was calm and focused as he flipped through page after page. He looked so intelligent. At that moment, he was definitely sane. It was as though I had caught a glimpse of an altogether different brother of mine, one who didn't touch alcohol. I still don't understand. By what coincidence my brother had ended up like that. Those few brief days were clearly set apart from the rest. It was as though he, whose life had taken a different road, had gotten lost somewhere along the way, ending up on an entirely different path. I wanted to demand answers. From whatever being out there that possessed a complete overview of the trajectory of my life. Why did you swap my brother, who had made so many mistakes, with that other version? What was the point of showing me that other brother? I've never told anyone about this mystical other brother of mine. Not even my mother. No matter how rigorous the words that I might try to use, they would never be enough to explain what I had seen. To explain it in sufficient detail, I would have to be a very morbid person indeed. So I decided not to think too deeply about them. Evidence, truth, that kind of thing. I filed it away as an undigested memory. A good memory. I will never forget my other brother's beauty. One day, I will tell someone about what I had seen. As a mere event. My listener will probably be amazed by how outlandish the story sounds. The story of my brother's death. Anyone who expects it to play out in order will no doubt be thrown off by the sudden appearance of this other version of him. The one traveling backward along the road to death.

They will probably think that I'm recounting events out of order. My brother was reading, something that he hardly ever did. I stepped into his room. And I interrupted him. He was normally so quick to lose his temper, but for some reason, he didn't get angry that day. He simply glanced up at me, and smiled. I'm reading *Emile*. It's really interesting. I'll lend it to you once I'm done. He said something like that. Out of the blue. Yes, completely out of the blue. One day, I will tell someone about the strange feeling that fell over me. That feeling of discomfort had no effect on me. There was no lesson to be learned. No meaning to that experience. When I tell people about it, I will only be able to relate it without attaching any sense of meaning. I will simply thrust them head-first into that world of discomfort.

After finishing that book, my brother went back to his life of drinking. Strangely, that didn't make me feel any sense of sorrow. And so, as though coming to the end of a summer vacation, that other version of my brother and I parted ways.

The woman and the youth arrived at Ōura Church. Urakami Cathedral was modern. Ōura Church, on the other hand, adhered to the conventional image of a Catholic church. There was an old woman sitting on a pew, praying fervently. The woman and the youth sat down some distance away from her.

This is the Basilica of the Holy Martyrs, isn't it? the woman said, pointing to a picture next to the cross. The painting showed twenty-six crosses in a row, each with a Japanese or foreign missionary hanging from it.

Yes, the youth answered. This church was built to commemorate martyred hidden Christians.

There are so many crosses lined up. I suppose there must be a connection to the number of the dead.

Do you know the etymology of the word *passion*?

The etymology? Of the English word? No.

Pathos. It's Greek.

Ah. . . Yes, now I remember. The English *passion* comes from the Greek *pathos*. I suppose it must mean something like *enthusiasm*, then?

Suffering. That's what it means.

Suffering?

That's right.

How strange. . . So the word *passion* was somehow derived from *suffering*? I wonder how that happened. Is a passionate person someone who has suffered? Maybe passions are a form of injury?

They say that joy and sorrow are both different kinds of suffering.

Suffering. . . I see.

The woman put her hands together. She stared up at the stained-glass ceiling for a while. Nostalgically. Tenderly. Then she spoke: I have a family. A husband, and a child. That kind of family.

I see. The youth placed his hand over hers.

We live in a small apartment complex, out in the suburbs. The kind of family you can find just about anywhere.

I thought so.

The woman and the youth looked at one another. The youth had an intelligent and discerning face. As though he knew all about the pathos that had brought the woman to this land. It had been like a typhoon approaching from afar. Deadly and violent. But then it had passed. Everything had returned to normal. Still. The same applied to these two people, who had loved one another so intensely. It was as though the youth had known this. As though he had known that he would inevitably lose this sexual love. Yes, he was supposed to have wept for the woman, to have indulged himself in pleasure to wipe away his sorrow. But it was as though he had fallen in love with her to ensure that he could leave her. Someone who could see far enough into the distance wouldn't have needed to take that detour. But he had innocently allowed her to play around with him. For what purpose? Who was he? Not even he knew.

The page turned from August ninth to August tenth, and the suffering along with it. August ninth was a day of absolute despair, but at the same time, it was somehow mystical. In the face of that mystery, the tenth was nothing short of mundane. The tenth, the eleventh, the twelfth. The same went for November fourteenth. Days devoid of mystery. The woman wondered. Just how mundane was this youth?

The youth forgave the woman. For what? For her blasphemy. The blasphemy of death. But the warning gaze that had frightened her probably wouldn't be directed her way again. She was still frightened. She was scared, because she couldn't see the youth's face. Because of the light shining behind him on the slope outside, she hadn't been able to make out his face as he fed bread to the dog. But now, in this church sanctuary where she had confessed about her family, she could stare hard into it. Into what it represented. Patience. He wouldn't punish her, momentarily or emotionally. He may well have had the power to do so. But he wouldn't. The woman was convinced of that. And she understood. That she had been forgiven. She was grateful. The youth had endured blasphemy during his time with her, as they engaged in intercourse. Death had become justice. Surely that had been the most degrading thing for him. He had affirmed suffering. The woman could see far into his future. There would be no end to his life. There would be no tragedy, no pleasure, no malice bordering on death. Those were suffering. He had left them behind. There was no eternal silence in him. Only eternal motion. The woman knew. That she was dramatically loved. But there was nothing that she could do about it. She was simply overwhelmed by the youth's strength. She could only watch the overflowing love of others from the sidelines. There was no love born in the woman's heart. The woman, her husband, and their child. Their small apartment complex in the suburbs. The woman would live there for a while. The memory of the youth, of his strong affirmation of life, would remain. She would live in awe of him. But she wouldn't be his faithful disciple. She would go on more dates with her husband. She would accept the suffering of despair. She would accept it as coequal to death. Easily.

But she no longer identified with anyone. Not with the youth, not with the child. Only she remained. Only she, alone.

Suffering, that tempest, raged around the woman, and left her in its wake. The past, the only man whom she had ever loved, the husband to whom she couldn't relate, the child whom she had thought still a part of herself, the greatest incident in the history of Nagasaki, the youth who had intersected with her in mind and in body, everything—all her sufferings were swept aside. Only the woman remained. Alone. In that place filled with nothing. Beside her sat the youth. The two of them turned toward one another. As though looking in a mirror. Their faces were so similar. Almost exactly alike. As though they were indeed the same person. But the woman was no longer confused. She could perceive the youth as someone else, someone too much like her. One who finds on the surface of a body of water the figure of another, a figure too similar to oneself, may end up throwing themself straight into it. That is the power of death. But the woman didn't. The death that had so fascinated her no longer dwelled inside her heart. The death of death. The destruction of death. Suffering engulfed the fortress of death, and reduced it to a sandy ruin. The woman touched the youth's face. Her heart was still. She touched the youth without any sense of desire. As though she were blind.

As though she could know that face only by touch. The youth's keen eyes grew moist, and for a moment, their brilliance was drowned out. He still loved her. The woman thought. That just as he had given bread to the dog, so too would he provide her with sustenance. That, as he had acted to stop her from dying, this man would no doubt offer her those crumbs of bread if she were hungry, even if it meant that he would starve in her place. The woman wasn't moved by this. A flower of grief blossomed inside her, and then fell away. The woman experienced the extinguishing of emotion. And so it ended, as a matter of course, like a sweater being knitted to completion. Was it the youth who had created this flow of time? Though accepting it like the sun's rays, the woman felt her emotions dry up in the face of the youth's great love. Winter, the four seasons, and the flow of time overtook that warm light. The woman was still young when she stopped feeling pleasure, when her senses grew numb. She had made herself into a corpse. Was she a corpse now, now that not only her joy, but her sorrow too had perished? She was but a cold cavity, a limestone cave. Quiet. Visited by no one. She had come to know this secret world of nothingness. She was what remained after facing the youth, his life-affirming, fulfilled existence, love still unconveyed. He had destroyed even death, leaving behind only nothingness.

Little by little, nothingness begins to speak of emotion. At first stuttering, but eventually growing fluent. Nothingness speaks. Nothingness is dressed in the symbols of words. The state of having spoken about nothing—*that* is nothing.

Matushka Lyubov owned a rich assortment of clothes. She had a different set for each Divine Liturgy, all of the highest quality. You could spot her at a glance. She stood out among all those members of the congregation who visited the cathedral. The clergy house and the cathedral were no more than a few meters apart, so why did she feel as though she needed to dress up like that? She never cut corners, not even for the Saturday evening services. For a mere two hours, she would don a brightly dyed dress that perhaps wasn't particularly suited for a cathedral setting. The other women, dressed in outfits that couldn't hold up to the Matushka's, would compliment one another on their choice of dress. No one ever complimented the Matushka.

The Matushka and her priest husband never went on holidays. Why then did she have so many beautiful outfits? It was as though she wore them simply to walk back and forth between the clergy house and the cathedral.

The priests dress in green robes on the day of the Pentecost. Green to symbolize the Holy Spirit. The Matushka likewise wore an emerald-green blouse as she participated in worship. Not a single member of the congregation took note of this. Even today, no one complimented the Matushka on her green blouse. The Matushka always stood by the Saint Sergius Chapel. A pregnant woman walked past the Matushka. She was wearing a dull printed dress. Not green.

The Matushka had no children. She didn't seem to be in good health. The Pentecost symbolizes life. A green womb standing by the Saint Sergius Chapel.

I once saw the Matushka perform an act of confession. She seemed to be crying. The priest began to whisper to her. They spoke for a long time. His tone of voice was strong. He seemed to be angry. I couldn't hear what he said, as his voice was drowned out by the singing of the choir. The Matushka nodded to the priest's words, occasionally wiping away her tears. Eventually, the Matushka knelt down in front of the analogion. The priest recited a prayer. The hem of her pale wisteria skirt spread out on the floor. A saint, a woman of Russian royalty, looked down on her.

My desire to talk about my family, my brother, my mother, and me, came out of nowhere. I don't know the true form of that desire. Just as we are forced to use pleonastic pronouns to describe good weather—instead of saying, for instance, that the sun is shining spontaneously in and of itself—so too was some pleonastic power driving that desire. What fell over me was the kind of thing that could only be described in terms of a word like *it*.

One day, in a calm moment that seemed to have nothing to do with emotion, *it* came to me. I wanted to tell my story, even if there wasn't anyone to listen. The story of my family would have no effect on the listener. No one would be moved to action. It wouldn't even move their heart. Once, a long time ago, I met a mysterious other version of my brother. The uncomfortable feeling of speaking, of putting *it* into words. That emptiness. It gradually eroded my past. Just as another version of my brother existed in my past, so too was another version of my mother mixed in, and another version of me. And that sense of discomfort didn't end with people. There was another sorrow, another place, another passage of time. The different perceptions of qualities inside me nested here and there amid the great tree of the past. I couldn't shake that feeling of discomfort, no matter how dramatic the moments of my past were when I talked about them. But no longer do I attempt to give order to what I once saw as the disorder of my past. It isn't possible to arrange a mix of letters from the alphabets of different countries into order.

I simply spread the obi of my past, dyed through with disorder and discomfort. I set the listener adrift on a sea of outlandishness. All that I can do is repeat this fruitless act. I don't hope for the possibility of healing or catharsis. There are no tears. I don't even feel a sense of despair over that fact.

How valuable is the life of a woman stalked by trivialities?

How many will remember what she had to say? What could she utter that would be of value? What is the purpose of these words? I speak. About my boring, daily life. Again and again. And that speech borders on silence.

I imagined sleeping with a man. Only the once. A man whom I had just met. We didn't know each other very well. That gentle but unreliable man inserted *it* into my vagina with trepidation. Once the act was over, we lay down on the bed. Like syrup. There were no boundaries between the bed and our bodies. Eventually, I began to speak. Quietly. Slowly. As though each word, even the smallest particle, was important. My mother can tell. When I've slept with a man, you know? The minute I walk through the door, she can tell. These words scared the man. He didn't want to make an enemy of my mother. He didn't want to be hated by someone whom he had never met before, whom he never would meet. Do you know why my mother says that? I asked. No, he replied with a serious expression. She doesn't like the idea of me sleeping with someone. And she's curious. She can't help herself. She wants to know everything about how young women have sex. Would he understand? Would this man, this person whom I had just met, be able to tell from something so superficial that my mother was a little strange? Your mother sounds a little odd, he said. An innocuous remark. Perhaps it was only natural. He didn't want to speak ill of the mother of the woman with whom he had just made love. My mother spoils my brother, but she's strict with me. It's a balancing act, I explained. That's a little weird, the man said. It doesn't really sound fair. The man was right. He didn't seem to have realized yet that unfairness is the norm in this world. My brother drinks like a drowning man. He sleeps with women. He smashes the furniture throughout the house. He does whatever he wants. And my mother can't stop him. Whenever my brother gets like that, she begs me to help. Stop him, please, she says. Why don't you just call the police? the man asked. If we did that, my brother would no doubt end up in a mental hospital. That's why my mother feels so sorry for him. She would feel terrible if he was locked up in a cell like that. I spoke of my mother's unfairness as though it made perfect sense. The man fell silent. Mute in the face of this unconvincing argument. The man didn't seem to be particularly bright. A dull man. He would probably never sleep with me again. He would probably think of me simply as a troublesome woman. Vaguely. Without being able to clarify the warped nature of my family. Because from his standpoint of irresponsibility, he had no obligation to think otherwise.

That was what I imagined. I speak to a man superficially about my family, and he leaves me. I've experienced it so many times. I couldn't stand it, the impossibility of speaking the truth. So many bitter memories. But now, I fall to wondering. Hasn't this act contributed to the transparency of my family, a family with neither meaning nor concept? Hasn't my own sense of anguish paralyzed me in some small way?

The woman and the youth were alone in the church. The old woman who had been praying earlier was gone. I want to know more about you, the youth said.

Well, it's so mundane. You say you want to hear about me, but I've never told anyone about my life until now. It was never worth telling anyone.

That's what I want to know more about.

The woman laughed. You're kind, she said. I'm happy to hear you say that, but I don't know what to say. There's so much. I don't know how to put it all in order.

Right. Well, in that case, how about this? You can tell me about the story of how a woman, you, and a certain man met and got married. I'm sure you'll realize once you get started. That it's a good story.

The woman felt small, and turned her gaze downward. We. . . she murmured. Quietly, she began to speak. We met at a small factory. A bookbindery. He was the factory manager. My job was accounting.

That must have been dramatic, two people from different departments meeting one another.

It wasn't necessarily dramatic. I sometimes had to work in the factory too. It wasn't a particularly big factory. Every now and then, it would get busy, and there wouldn't be enough people to get everything done, so I would have to help out. Well, with odd jobs, I mean.

Tell me more about them, those odd jobs.

You can't leave everything to machines in a bookbinding factory, you know? All the machines are good for is binding the paper and trimming the margins. The papers have to be arranged by hand, from first to last. Pretty primitive, no. . .? You don't think this is boring?

It's fine. Keep going.

It gets busiest toward the end of the academic and fiscal years. There's always a rush of orders for graduation books and albums. That's when the accounting staff has to help out in the factory. Lining up all the papers. We have to stay up all night. Of course, that night, the factory manager—my husband now—was busy working too. That was how we met. We had all kinds of conversations while we laid out the papers. That was how we got to know each other.

What did you talk about?

Oh, nothing much. Just the usual things.

Like what?

The woman pressed her hand against her forehead in embarrassment. At first, it was just the weather. The rain was depressing, he said. I always thought rain was romantic, but when he said that, I ended up agreeing with him. Do you know what I mean?

I know exactly what you mean.

After that, we moved onto talking about recent baseball games, and then our hobbies. He likes all kinds of sports. I don't have any hobbies. I told him I just liked to wander the streets at night. He laughed. I thought he hated me. But the next time I worked overtime, he asked me out on a date.

It's a good story.

The woman fell silent. A smoke-like sadness passed over her. She caught hold of the youth's consideration for a brief second, like a fish in a river, and let it go. It wasn't something that she was supposed to know. She had to keep talking, act as though she hadn't realized anything. She shouldn't have said anything important. On the surface, hers was a happy family. She should have spoken only about the surface. The fact that this happy woman had come to this land captivated by an image of a mushroom cloud was something that had to be forgotten.

The two of them continued talking for a while. A pleasant, organic sorrow that she had never before known enveloped her.

A story about love affirms existence. How helpless we all are. What is this gulf between existence and the self? I see that affirmation from a distance. There is no affirmation of myself yet. But I can't see my own death anymore either. There is no end to the madness that transcends madness, to this desire to speak. Experiences seeking recognition through the power of words. False recognition. Mere delusions. I spit them out. They are too much. And now, they are depleted. Consumed to exhaustion. Like spent air after being exhaled. The oxygen has been absorbed, leaving behind only nitrogen. A nothingness by relation. And as I spit out this near-nothingness, I forget my despair. I don't know why. My despair, which I had blindly considered beautiful, had drawn too heavily on symbols, had been expressed too inaccurately. I did it again, and again. And that act neutralized even my despair. What kind of miracle keeps a person barely alive in a world filled with phenomena that are impossible to give form?

The woman returned. To her home, to her small flat in an apartment complex in the suburbs. It was still afternoon, but her husband was at home. He had taken a break from work to look after the child, he explained. I was worried about you, he murmured. You left without saying anything, and you weren't at your mother's place either. I waited, but I was going to file a missing person's report with the police today. I'm sorry, the woman said, before rushing to the apartment next door, to her pregnant neighbor with whom she had left her child.

Her neighbor stood at the door, her hands pressed against her protruding belly. The woman apologized for having left the child with her. I'm sorry. My mother fell ill and collapsed, so I had to rush out. Her neighbor accepted this lie, complete with all its contradictions. Or at least she acted as though she did. I don't mind, she said. My husband and I had a great time with him. We love kids.

The woman gave her husband and child some souvenirs. A glass poppen toy and a castella cake for the child. A bottle of Saga sweet potato shōchū for her husband. Not Nagasaki shōchū. Her husband stared at the label, then at the child's poppen and castella cake. Did you go to Kyushu? he asked. Yes, the woman flashed him a forced smile. A bus tour around Kyushu.

Why? her husband asked, watching her with kind eyes. Why would you go there all of a sudden? And without even telling anyone? The woman searched for an answer. The child blew into the poppen. No sound came out. Well, actually, it wasn't supposed to be me. A friend of mine booked the trip, but she got a fever all of a sudden, so I bought her ticket off her and went in her place.

What's this toy? the child asked. You blow in it, and it makes a sound, the woman answered. No it doesn't. It's boring. The woman set the child on her lap. There's a trick to it, she said. A trick? the child asked. What's a trick? An easy way to do it. Any easy way to make a sound? You have to hold your breath, and blow it into the tube. With those instructions, the child started blowing into the poppen again.

Is there a trick to drinking sweet potato shōchū too? her husband asked with a laugh. You don't need to add plums or tea or anything to it, the woman answered. You can just serve it with ice, or hot water. That's all you need. The woman smiled.

Maybe we should have a drink? Her husband went to look in the freezer. It's a little early for dinner, the woman laughed, frightened. Her husband wasn't the kind of man who drank while it was still light out. Nor was he the kind to drink to an unhealthy excess. Why don't you tell me about your trip over a glass? he murmured softly.

Two glasses filled with ice. He poured the shōchū into each of them. Cheers, he said, lifting his into the air. The evening light illuminated his face. A speaker blared from an organic vegetable delivery truck that had just arrived outside. The child still couldn't make a sound with the poppen. The two of them brought their glasses together with a clink.

This apartment building sure is noisy, her husband said. His eyes narrowed, the corners of his lips lifting in a slight smile. As though he were testing her. I'd like to get a house, if we can afford it. I heard the emergency alarm malfunctioned the day that you left, right?

Oh. Yes, the woman replied blandly. Feigning indifference. I'm satisfied here. That new shopping mall nearby opened two years ago, remember? It's made life so much easier. It has everything. Not just a supermarket. A movie theater, a large toy store, even a restaurant area. I bought your windbreaker there. Really, it has everything.

I don't like it here, her husband murmured. All these people squeezed into one place. All these shops bunched together. Where I grew up, near my parents' place, the shops are spread throughout a large shopping district. And there are public baths and parks everywhere. So it's kind of stifling for me here. The people will probably revolt one day. Wasn't there a bit of an uproar when the emergency alarm went off?

Well, it was right around the time of day when all us housewives are getting dinner ready. Everyone has a lot of free time on their hands around that time, you know? You aren't busy nonstop when you're cooking, you know? There's time to watch TV while it's simmering on the stove. But housewives aren't interested in the kind of news they show on TV. That's when the emergency alarm rang. That alarm was the biggest news of the day. Everyone sprang to action at that sound. And after they went outside and made sure there wasn't an earthquake or a fire, they all gathered around the malfunctioning alarm.

Such a fuss over a broken alarm. Housewives sure must be starved for conversation, her husband said in bewilderment. That's just it, the woman answered with a laugh.

A few days later, the woman suggested to her husband that they go into Tokyo. Where in Tokyo? he asked. An amusement park? No, the woman answered. A place called Surugadai. There's a big church there. I heard it was restored a few years ago, so I want to see it. Did you ever see it before then? Yes. My school was nearby. I stopped there sometimes on my way home.

Alright, her husband said, resting a hand on her head. I'll go with you, anywhere you want. So don't go off alone without saying anything again, okay?

The woman, her husband, and their child passed through

the gate of the Tokyo Holy Resurrection Cathedral by the old Russian school. A young man wearing a black cassock stepped out from the building, greeting them. Was he a priest? the woman's husband asked her. A seminary student, the woman answered. That building looks like it's still a seminary.

Her husband spotted a foggy glass window. I wonder what that is. A sauna? he asked. That's where they make the sacramental bread, the woman answered. You sure know a lot about this place, her husband commented. The woman laughed.

It was almost time for the cathedral to open for worship. The child wanted to offer a candle, so they bought three. Without understanding anything about it, the child said that he wanted to place his in front of an acheiropoieton. The woman lifted the child up near the candles. She couldn't offer a candle to the Weeping Theotokos. It had been closed off behind a rope, and she couldn't approach it.

Mama, who's the person in the picture? the child asked. She explained simply that it was God. He asked who the others were. They're God's disciples, the woman answered. Everyone's wearing such fancy clothes. Are they vestments? her husband asked. Yes, the woman answered.

Mama, that person's aren't fancy, the child said, pointing to the Saint Sergius Chapel. That's Alexius, a Holy Fool and Venerable. He's dressed in rags. Why is he dressed like that? the child asked. I don't know, the woman answered.

The metropolitan archdiocese office. Icons and crosses were being sold there. A small store. The woman's husband went to look at the crosses, and suggested buying one for her. Maybe, the woman answered indifferently as she looked over the church bulletin. She startled when she laid eyes on a photograph accompanying one of the articles, a picture of the youth whom she had met in Nagasaki, garbed in the robes of a subdeacon. The article explained that the Metropolitan had attended the commemoration of Saint Seraphim of Sarov in

Russia, accompanied by two priests and a subdeacon who had acted as an interpreter.

The event was held in a rural area, seven hundred and fifty kilometers east of Moscow, a distance of ten hours by train. On the first day, the hut where the saint had lived was reconstructed. On the second day, after a congratulatory speech by the president, a crucession was held to transfer the immortal body of the saint from Sarov to Diveyevo. On the third day, the Divine Liturgy was held.

The article concluded by saying that the author felt honored to have participated in the commemoration of his patron saint, Saint Seraphim. It had been written by the youth.

What's wrong? the woman's husband asked. He glanced at the church bulletin. Is there something interesting in it?

No, the woman answered. No, it's nothing. I just used to drop by here a lot when I was a student. It made me feel nostalgic.

Her husband again offered to buy her a cross. The woman shook her head. It's alright. There's nothing else I need to do here. Nothing at all.

The woman missed the anonymity of the youth. She called for him. Nagasaki. As though he himself were that tragedy. But now, the woman knew his true name. Seraphim. The loss of that anonymity had torn the two of them apart. The woman would continue to live as a housewife in a small apartment complex. She had unmistakably witnessed a person with a name. But this experience hadn't allowed her to give a name to herself. Nonetheless, she would no doubt weep, one day, over her memories of Nagasaki, over that time spent with another person. Would she think of that version of herself as unhappy? That version of herself who hadn't been capable of weeping, because she was already dead? Would she think of herself as unhappy, having forgotten the past that had made her feel that way?

I stare at the photograph. A picture of me, my brother, and my mother. In the photograph, my brother is wearing an artistic smile, a smile with a brilliant sense of perception. My mother is flexing her facial muscles in disgust at the camera. The three people in this photograph don't know it yet. What would happen to their minds in the future. But I think to myself that I will write, someday. A novel. Me, my brother, and my mother. A community comprised of the self and others. I will write it as a love story between a woman and a man. Someday, like a river. Is my goal loss, forfeiture? My work will flow so smoothly that people will think that it must be. I will deplete the power of the words, consume them to exhaustion, until they render me transparent.